Lost in his eyes

Winston held out his arm to gesture for her to sit down. Susannah tripped on a tree root and tumbled. Winston moved fast. He caught her in his arms.

She found herself staring at his cravat. He held her in a firm embrace against his chest. Now, the one time she did not wish to be close to him, her clumsiness had forced her into his arms. Susannah cleared her throat and looked up.

A hint of a smile tugged at the corners of his mouth. Winston knew she was not nearly as graceful as she should be, but it amused rather than embarrassed him. The interesting part was that he had not let go of her.

Susannah was sorely tempted to stay in his arms, but knew that she needed to discuss his mysterious secret before she let her feelings for him have their way. She needed a clear head today, so she pulled out of his embrace.

"Are you all right?" he whispered.

"Fine," she said quickly. Too quickly. But she was nervous. She was not sure she wanted to hear what Winston had to say. What if it changed how she felt about him?

The Captain's Secret

Jenna Mindel

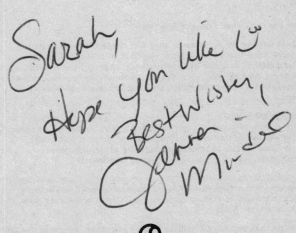

Sarah,
Hope you like it
Best Wishes,
Jenna Mindel

A SIGNET BOOK

SIGNET
Published by New American Library, a division of
Penguin Putnam Inc., 375 Hudson Street,
New York, New York 10014, U.S.A.
Penguin Books Ltd, 80 Strand,
London WC2R 0RL, England
Penguin Books Australia Ltd, Ringwood,
Victoria, Australia
Penguin Books Canada Ltd, 10 Alcorn Avenue,
Toronto, Ontario, Canada M4V 3B2
Penguin Books (N.Z.) Ltd, 182–190 Wairau Road,
Auckland 10, New Zealand

Penguin Books Ltd, Registered Offices:
Harmondsworth, Middlesex, England

First published by Signet, an imprint of New American Library,
a division of Penguin Putnam Inc.

First Printing, October 2002
10   9   8   7   6   5   4   3   2   1

To my friend and sister, Lisa, who introduced me to the world of writing long ago when I'd sneak into her room and read the wonderful stories she had written. Thank you for being an example of excellence.

I love you!

Prologue

S usannah Lacey walked with Captain Winston Jef- fries to the shore of the small lake. Her arm rested lightly on his. She was nervous. She feared she would cry but knew that would only make matters worse. She had to be brave for his sake. They strolled along in silence until finally Captain Jeffries turned to her.

"Susannah." He looked into her eyes with a seri- ousness she had seen only briefly before. "I want you to know that I will carry the memory of our friendship and these past few days together into battle with me. It will keep me safe."

She felt a lump of emotion threaten to close her throat. She swallowed twice before she trusted herself to speak. "My prayers and those of my family go with you, Winston." It was the first time she had called him by his Christian name. "That will keep you safe and bring you back to me."

"Thank you, but, Susannah, you mustn't wait for me. You are young with your whole life ahead of you. There are many young gentlemen yet to meet. Prom- ise me that you will have your Season, whether it be in Bath or London." He took her hand. "Promise me that you will flirt with all your suitors until you find a rich and worthy man to take care of you for the rest of your life." His voice was soft and full of emotion, like that of a man who expected to die.

Her eyes welled up with tears. One tear escaped to run down her cheek. "Do not worry for me," she whispered. She did not care how long it took or how long he was gone, she would wait for him. Despite her sixteen years, she knew her heart. Captain Winston Jeffries was the only man for her.

"Promise me," he insisted.

She sniffed. "I promise I shall have my Season."

He nodded, satisfied with her answer. He reached into his waistcoat pocket and pulled out a stickpin, one a gentleman would wear in his cravat. It was a small butterfly encrusted with tiny diamonds and rubies. He offered it to her. "I want you to have this. My brother, who tries to make a proper gentleman out of me, gave it to me. I cannot wear such a feminine thing. Please take it and think kindly of me when you look upon it."

She cradled the pin in her hands before she affixed it to her dress, just below the shoulder. "It is beautiful. Thank you, I shall treasure it always."

He shrugged his shoulders, as if she made him uncomfortable by treating his gift with such reverence. "A trifle really," he said.

She wondered what she could give him in return, when an idea struck her. "You must have something of mine as well."

"Susannah, you do not have to give me anything."

"But I do." She reached back and snatched a hat pin from her bonnet. It was made entirely of paste jewels, but it sparkled with prisms of blue and gold. "You may feel funny carrying around a lady's hat pin.

It is not nearly as grand, but perhaps you might use it as a weapon." She let out a giggle despite her tears.

"A wonderful idea." He smiled broadly as he took the hat pin, and settled it into the material of his red cavalry coat.

"And think of me when you carry it." She gazed into his eyes.

"I will." He looked away and kicked at the grass with his foot. He looked up at the darkening sky with an air of defeat. "Susannah, I must go."

"I know." Her heart felt like it was ready to break in two. She knew his reluctance to leave had much to do with his fear of returning to war. She also believed that he did not wish to leave her.

"Do take care," he said. He took her hand and raised it to his lips for the briefest of kisses.

"And you do the same." She reminded herself to be brave, but her insides quaked.

He caressed her cheek and then he walked away.

Susannah watched his long strides take him away from her. "Do be sure and write to us," she called after him with a strained voice.

He turned and waved with a smile. She forced herself to wave in return, but her heart had never felt so heavy. She stood alone for what seemed like an eternity, her throat dry and tight with the sob that she had been holding down. She silently begged God to keep him safe.

Chapter One

*S*usannah Lacey sat down at her desk and sighed. The three letters written to her from Captain Winston Jeffries almost three years ago lay before her. She had been only sixteen when they met, but age had not changed what was in her heart. She could not read the letters without experiencing the inevitable pain that lodged itself in her soul. She had clipped a list of the soldiers fallen in battle at Toulouse from the *Morning Post* two years ago, and that list slid out from the pages of the last letter Winston had sent her. He had been listed among the wounded, but she had never heard from him. She wondered for the hundredth time what had happened to him.

Surely if he had lived, Winston would have written to her. But then perhaps, he simply did not wish to see her again. Perhaps, he did not return the love that she felt still. Was she nursing an impossible hope that he was alive? If so, she had to stop. For whatever reason, Winston had not sought her out. She had to accept that. She had to move on with her life. She hoped for children one day, but she would never realize that goal if she continued to pine after a memory.

Winston no doubt had viewed her only as the child she had been. Winston had made her promise to have a Season when they said good-bye, and finally, she would.

Lady Evelyn Abbott, her dear sister's mother-in-law, sponsored her come-out along with the help of Susannah's Aunt Agatha. She was not about to worry any of them with a show of the dismals.

"Miss Susannah?" Botts, the young maid assigned to her, stepped into her bedchamber.

"Yes?"

"There has been a change in plans. Your aunt and Lady Evelyn have decided that a trip to the theater would be the very thing this evening. Lord and Lady Sheldrake have just arrived."

Susannah smiled. Aunt Agatha simply wanted to be gone from the bustle and noise of Jane, a very boisterous three-year-old, and her cantankerous infant brother, George. Susannah doted on her niece and nephew, but they could be overly loud when introduced to new surroundings. Lord Sheldrake, her brother-in-law, did not wish to leave his family behind when he attended Parliament. And so, he had leased a veritable mansion in Mayfair to house them all for the Season.

She rose to her feet and nearly tripped on her gown. She followed Botts to the armoire. Her bedchamber was large with considerable light and an excellent view of the street below from two tall windows. "What should I wear this evening, do you think?" Susannah asked her maid.

Botts whisked through the newly hung gowns before pulling out a celestial blue confection with a silvery net overlay. Botts, though young, had been well trained.

"This I think. Such color is fine for Drury Lane."

Susannah nodded in agreement. Once dressed with her hair coiffed into a near perfect halo of riotous golden curls, she was ready. And then she remembered. "My pin." Susannah rushed to the box containing her modest but excellent array of jewels. She pulled out a stickpin with a small butterfly encrusted with rubies and diamonds. She hastened to attach it to her dress, just below her shoulder, right above her heart.

Botts did not approve. "It does not match."

"Yes, it does." Susannah stood before the mirror, inwardly cursing herself for her weakness. She had worn this pin everyday for three years. It was time to put it aside. She knew that. How could she look for a husband and give the poor man half of a chance, if she kept holding onto Winston's memory? Her fingers shook as she carefully unfastened the pin and put it back in the box. "I suppose you are correct."

She followed her maid out with a feeling of emptiness. She knew she must stop nursing hope to see Winston again. Even so, it hurt terribly.

Captain Winston Jeffries, toweled and dry from his bath, stood inspecting his newly purchased black evening coat and linens. He had been cooling his heels for days in London, awaiting direction from the Office of Foreign Affairs for his next assignment. After finally receiving those directions, he found himself in a nice kettle of fish. Lord Castlereagh, the foreign secretary, had described the intricacies of his duty to perfection. He completely understood his goal. He knew his plan of attack, but he did not have to like it.

Playing the gallant admirer to a whey-faced chit in order to find proof that her papa was a traitor was not his style. He would do what he must for king and country. If he succeeded, he just might receive the post he wanted in India. He rubbed his chin as he stared at his sadly lacking wardrobe. This mission meant the purchase of many things he'd rather not have to spend his blunt upon. He needed clothes befitting his station, an experienced valet, and a fashionable address with a decent stable.

He let out an irritated sigh and tried to think of the positive side of things. He had been given a rather nice sum from the Foreign Office to use, but it was not nearly enough. Someday, when he was settled in India and living in peace, it would all be worth it. Either way, after this mission, he wanted out. He was done with finding traitors to the crown.

He applied a modest amount of cologne and reached for his shirt only to catch a glimpse of his torso in the looking glass. The sight of the long thin scar from a saber wound he received at Toulouse two years ago, still caused his stomach to knot with regret. If only he had gotten out of the way, he might have been left to captain his dragoons. Perhaps then he would never have been approached by the austere Lord Castlereagh to work for the Foreign Office. His gaze rested on his scarred left hand, and his frown deepened. No matter how far away he ran, his hand remained a constant reminder of his sins. Turning away from his image, he shrugged into the shirt.

Lucky for him this contrived courtship for a pretend bride was merely playacting. He had no desire to woo a maid. How could he possibly explain what kept him up at night, or what made him tremble and sweat when he did catch a few precious hours of sleep? Such madness was reason enough for Winston to keep his distance from the fair sex.

In no time he sauntered down the stairs of Stephen's Hotel on Bond Street, where he had spent his last three nights. He fished out of his pocket the calling card of the man he had been told to meet this evening at the Royal Theater on Drury Lane. Winston wore a red rose pinned to his lapel as instructed. Castlereagh had said that this man, Lord Ponsby, would introduce him to polite society and steer him in the direction of his target; a Miss Caroline Dunsford.

Whistling under his breath, he walked the few blocks and entered the theater amid glittering ladies and noblemen. He made his way through the crowd when suddenly a hand grasped his elbow. He looked into the face of a man with shrewd blue eyes, and surprisingly young years.

"Captain Jeffries, I presume," the gentleman said.

Winston turned to the man. "Yes, and you, sir?"

"Why, Lord Ponsby of course. I have been expecting you. Come, follow me to my box where we can get better acquainted."

Winston followed quietly until they were seated in a lavish box with an excellent view of the stage. He would have expected something far off toward the wall.

"Are you comfortable? May I offer you a pinch of snuff?" Ponsby leaned toward him with a jeweled-toned box in his outstretched hand.

"No, I thank you," Winston said. "A bit in the open, wouldn't you say? Are you not concerned about being overheard?"

Ponsby waved his hand in dismissal. "I shall go straight to the matter. I have here of list of parties, routs, dinners and the like to which I will ensure your invitation." He handed it to Winston. "Take care in responding to every single one with acceptance. My

sister will put your name about as a well-to-do captain
back from the wars. Your lineage is respectable, I
have already checked. We should have no trouble at
all, passing you off as a desirable young man in search
of a good match. All doors of society will be opened
to you."

Winston nodded. There was no stopping what he
was about to become. His sudden appearance would
have to be explained in order to gain such high entrée
among the *ton*. He was grateful for someone like Lord
Ponsby to smooth his way. "I understand there is a
lady that I must court. How shall I seek her out?"

"Leave that to me. I will introduce you to Miss
Dunsford at my sister's rout in three days. But we
shall meet again before then," Ponsby said.

The theater was now full. The lights had dimmed
to announce the start of the play. He leaned back in
his chair, eagerly awaiting the curtain's opening. He
looked around. The faces of high society blurred before his eyes until a blaze of diamonds suddenly
caught his attention.

"Hey, Ponsby, who's that over there looking like
royalty?"

Ponsby appeared a bit irritated at Winston's informal use of his name, but looked about to see of whom
he referred. "I am assuming you mean the young lady
wearing the tiara?"

Winston did not for a minute mistake the insolent
drawl in the other man's voice. "Yes, that's the one."

"That is Princess Esterhazy, one of the patronesses
of Almack's." Lord Ponsby nodded politely when she
caught his gaze. "You would do well to ingratiate
yourself with her and Lady Cowper and Lady Jersey.
They rule over Almack's."

"All guardians of the hallowed halls, eh?"

"Indeed. Have you never attended society functions in London, my boy?"

This time it was Winston's turn to bristle with indignation. At twenty-nine, he was hardly a boy, no more so than the stiff-necked Ponsby. "Quite frankly, it all seems like a bit of fluff and nonsense to me. I have had my schedule rather full fighting a war."

Ponsby had the grace to color slightly. "Indeed. I will ensure that you meet whom you must. It is after all a matter of national security."

"Indeed." Winston copied the other man's term and then, with good humor, winked at him to show that he held no hard feelings toward him. Had Winston's elder brother not been maimed in a farming accident, the two might have made more trips to London simply for social visits. But that hadn't been the case, and as much as his brother had tried to make a gentleman of fashion out of him, Winston had balked at the effort. Winston was a military man. That had always been good enough.

Tapping his foot with impatience for the play to begin, Winston gazed about the boxes again. The crowd cared more about being seen than the rising of the curtain. He noticed an angel perched upon the edge of her seat as she eagerly awaited the start of the play. She checked a dainty timepiece she wore and then her playbook. Her identity suddenly hit him like cannon fire. By all that was holy, it was Susannah Lacey!

Dread, regret, and desire filled him at once, and his heart felt like it had fallen into the soles of his feet. Her hair was different. She had cut it, and it fell in a riot of curls about her head. She was different—no, she had simply grown up. He sat there, his gaze riveted to the one female he had tried to forget. The woman he thought that he would never see again was sitting five opera boxes away from him.

Surely, she must have married by now, he thought. Panic settled over him. What if she attended the same parties as he? How would he address her if he came face-to-face with her? The theater was near dark but for the lights from the stage.

The soft light shining on Susannah's face wreaked havoc with his insides. As he watched her, bittersweet memories of a military leave spent in her company clouded his mind. Without thought, he reached into the inside pocket of his coat and pulled out the hat pin she had given him the day he left her. It was a sweet reminder of more innocent days when he was merely an idealistic soldier. He twirled it between his fingers, and wondered what the deuce he would say to her when she found out he was alive.

"I say, Captain. Are you listening?"

Ponsby's voice intruded, and Winston sat up straight. "What's that?"

"I asked if you knew her."

"Knew who?" He replaced the pin.

"Why, the golden beauty in the box over there. You have been staring at her this age."

Winston felt uncomfortable. "I met her a long time ago," he murmured.

"Perhaps we should pay a visit to their box . . ."

"No!"

Something in Winston's tone must have given Ponsby pause, since he said nothing more.

Winston noticed with irritation that now Ponsby watched her as well. Lord Ponsby was the type of man he supposed most of the young ladies would find agreeable. Handsome and more reserved in manner and dress than the typical London dandy, Ponsby carried himself well. If his tailoring was any indication, he was well to grass, and just the sort of man Susannah's beauty could attract.

Surely she would have married, he thought. She was nineteen by now. She would not have waited for him, would she have? Winston shifted uncomfortably and guilt gnawed at his insides. He had never bothered to find out. Finally, he tore his gaze away from her and watched the stage.

The lights brightened to announce an intermission, and Susannah stood to stretch her legs. The play was fine, but being part of the audience was more thrilling as she looked around. There was an exhilarating tension in the crowd that was a tangible thing. Everyone nearly hummed in anticipation of the Season to commence.

"Are you enjoying this evening's production, dear?" Aunt Agatha asked.

"Completely."

"Charming is it not?" Lady Evelyn added.

"Charming," Susannah agreed. She turned to watch people as they weaved in and out of boxes. She noticed a center box where two finely dressed gentlemen stood, one with his back to her. The other gentleman caught her looking and tipped his head in acknowledgment. He had the polished good looks of a man about town, sophisticated and all knowing. He was the type of man she should be interested in meeting, but she felt nothing.

With a sigh, she looked away, but not before she caught the profile of the other man. Her heart skittered to a halt, and her blood rushed to her head making her feel dizzy. It could not be! Taking a deep breath to lend her courage, she looked again. The gentleman turned around and faced her. It was Winston!

Her gaze swept down as much of his body as she could see. It was her very own Captain Winston Jeffries, and he appeared to be quite whole! She looked directly into his eyes. He recognized her as well. Her knees gave out, and she landed with an ungraceful drop into her chair. She did not know what to do or how to react. She merely stared at him as if he were a ghost. But he was no ghost. Winston Jeffries was alive and quite well.

"Susannah." Her aunt tapped her shoulder. "Susannah, are you all right, dear? You have gone completely pale."

"He's alive," she whispered.

"What did you say?"

Susannah shook her head to clear it. "Nothing. Aunt Agatha, I need to take some air."

"It is rather warm in here. Come, I will go with you, but let us tell Lady Evelyn."

Susannah got up from her chair on shaking legs and followed her aunt down the staircase. Once outside, she leaned against the railing and breathed deeply of the cool night air. It gave her some relief from her distress. She stood silent, knowing her aunt was concerned, but grateful that she did not press her with questions.

After a long while, her aunt placed her hand upon Susannah's shoulder and asked with concern, "Better?"

"Completely," Susannah lied. Her heart was breaking all over again. Why had he not written to let her know he was alive?

"Very well. We had best return to our seats before the second half of the play begins."

She took her aunt's proffered arm, and together they went back inside. As they climbed the stairs, Winston and the gentleman with him in the box were coming down. She looked up in time to see Winston stop in midstep. He looked like a rabbit ready to dart away if she made any threatening moves. Her breath caught in her throat, and she suddenly felt sick, but she forced herself into a modicum of calm. She would not fall to pieces in front of him. "Captain, how good to see you looking so well," she said.

A faint blush of color rose to his cheeks. "Miss Lacey, and Miss Wilts. I am honored to see you both again." He bowed.

Susannah caught her aunt looking from her to Winston and back at her. Aunt Agatha's mouth had fallen slightly open.

"Leaving the theater so soon?" Susannah was surprised at how cool her voice had become.

"Yes."

He was running away, she thought, like he had done years before. But that was not quite true—he had a war to return to. They stood for a moment, staring awkwardly at each other, when the sophisticated gentleman cleared his throat.

"I beg your pardon," Winston said. "Lord Ponsby, may I present Miss Susannah Lacey and her aunt, Miss Wilts. Ladies, Lord Ponsby."

"Miss Wilts, Miss Lacey, delighted." Lord Ponsby took Aunt Agatha's hand and bowed over it. Then he captured Susannah's hand and placed a discreet kiss slightly above her gloved fingers.

"We were just heading to Ponsby's club," Winston added hurriedly.

"Please." Susannah stepped aside. "Do not let us keep you."

Winston hurried down the stairs, leaving an offended Lord Ponsby, who appeared hesitant to move, standing uncomfortably alone. "I am sure that we shall meet again. Ladies, your servant." He bowed gracefully, then followed Winston.

Susannah gathered her scattered wits and emotions. Aunt Agatha had finally closed her mouth. "I thought the captain was dead."

"Yes, well, he is obviously very much alive." She could not hide the pain.

Her aunt wrapped her arm around Susannah's shoulders and gave her a quick squeeze. "I am sorry, my dear."

"So am I," she said with a sigh. Her reply sounded ridiculous to her ears, almost as if she regretted that the captain had lived. But that was not it at all. She had prepared herself for the worst, for death.

She followed her aunt up the stairs and into their private box as the curtains on stage rose for the last acts. The play had lost its allure. Susannah sat demurely with her hands gently folded in her lap, but her insides waged a private war between heartache and anger. The longer she thought about what had just taken place, how Winston had dashed away with no explanation, the more anger took the upper hand. By the end of the play, she was fairly fuming with bitter rage. She would find out why Winston deemed it appropriate to leave her wondering about him for three long years.

Winston climbed into Ponsby's plush carriage, grateful that Ponsby had agreed to leave the theater and even more grateful that the man stayed silent during the short trip to White's. Winston kept seeing Susannah's pale face when she had recognized him. Although she had remained calm when they met face-to-face, she was deeply upset. He did not blame her. Seeing her again had upset everything in his already erratic world.

Three years ago, she had been a girl just out of the schoolroom and much too young to trifle with her affections. But of course he *had* trifled with them. She had fallen in love with him. He had loved her in return even though he had never let on to that fact.

"Awfully quiet you are, Captain Jeffries. Are you sure you are up to it?"

"Up to what?"

"White's, man."

"Of course I am. I need to understand these *ton* popinjays enough to infiltrate their ranks."

Ponsby visibly took insult to this statement, but instead of raising a huff, he narrowed his gaze. "Seeing Miss Lacey has caused you discomfort."

"Yes," Winston answered, then thought better of opening up to him. "No. I was merely surprised to see her is all."

"What is she to you?"

Winston did not like the question, nor did he expect such a proper gentleman to ask something so personal. Perhaps Ponsby was more solid than he had given him credit for. "She is nothing, merely an acquaintance. A friend of a friend," he lied.

Ponsby only nodded his head. "Indeed."

The carriage slowed to a stop as they pulled in front of White's. Ponsby exited first. Winston followed. He looked forward to a bit of male company and a glass of port to wipe away the memory of Susannah's expression of heartbreak.

They entered the club, which was quite full of lounging gentlemen smoking cheroots or indulging in fine spirits. Here Winston felt at ease. The air smelled of smoke and the remains of cooked roast. As they made their way to a table, Winston nodded to some acquaintances from cavalry days. Port was served. He had come here with Ponsby for a reason. He needed to learn all he could about the *ton*.

The two men sat near the bowed window, with its view overlooking St. James Street. They were served immediately. Winston took a sip of port.

Ponsby narrowed his gaze before he said, "You should buy your clothes from Weston's. Although the coat you wear is fine, it looks to be a few seasons old."

Winston thought his coat completely satisfactory. "I have just purchased this."

"At a discount, I hope." Ponsby smiled.

Winston had much to learn.

"Let that be your first lesson," Ponsby said. "You must dress the part of a rich man, which means the latest style. As to manners . . ."

Winston cocked an eyebrow. "Are you afraid that I will embarrass you, Ponsby?" Winston was a gentleman after all. He knew how to behave.

"What I was about to say," Ponsby soothed, "is that you are fine there."

Winston felt properly chastised. He would give this young lord his attention and learn what he could. He knew little of London's upper ten thousand. The only trips he had made to Town were for military matters or Foreign Office assignments. He had never thought the *haute monde* was important. Until now.

"You are rather peevish. Castlereagh warned me," Ponsby said.

"Forgive me," Winston said. "Go on, tell me what I need to know."

"Actually, I have just thought of an idea. My sister

is having a small dinner party tomorrow night. You shall come with me. It is much easier to get to know some of the rulers of society if you can meet them in an intimate setting. You are a handsome fellow. You will be remembered and no doubt talked about for days among the ladies. It is perfect, the perfect introduction."

"Your sister will not mind?" Winston had hoped to have a couple more days to prepare, to buy the things he needed to impress Miss Dunsford.

"Not at all. You will mess up her even number of guests, but that is of no consequence."

"Will this Miss Dunsford be there?"

"No."

"Very well, then, I will go." Winston took another sip of port.

Chapter Two

Susannah sat next to her sister, Olivia, in the Sheldrake carriage as they turned onto the lane heading north to Hampstead. The methodical clack of the horses' hooves echoed in Susannah's ears. She wished that Aunt Agatha had not said a word about Winston. But of course she had. Susannah sat calmly while Olivia and Sheldrake drilled her with questions.

"Did he tell you why he has not written to you in nigh three years?" Olivia asked.

"He did not. As I told you before, we spoke only for a moment. Captain Jeffries and another gentleman were on their way to their club." Susannah kept her back straight, her voice even.

"I see," her sister murmured.

Susannah did not miss the glance that Olivia exchanged with her husband who merely frowned. "It is nothing, so if you please, do not worry about it." Susannah tried her best to sound cheerful, but failed. "I am grown now, and fully capable of handling the situation on my own." There, she thought, that should send the message that the subject of Winston Jeffries was closed.

Again, Olivia and her husband exchanged concerned looks, but they kept quiet.

"Tell me again. Where are we going?" Susannah

asked in an attempt to lighten the heavy mood that had settled inside of the carriage.

"This morning the Earl of Yarmouth invited Richard and myself to his home in Hampstead for dinner. They are having a small gathering. Since you are nearly *out*, Richard asked if you might join us. And so here you are."

"Do you know this earl well?" Susannah asked Sheldrake.

"Not so well, but he and I often see eye to eye on issues raised at Parliament. We have formed a friendship of sorts over it. He is called Lord Derne."

"I see," Susannah said as she turned to look out of the carriage window.

They arrived at Lord and Lady Derne's estate to join the line of carriages pulled into the drive. Candlelight twinkled from the windows, and Susannah had to own that she was nervous. This was her first real social gathering, and she wanted to make a good impression.

Entering the vast entrance hall, Susannah was hard-pressed not to gawk at the extravagance surrounding her. Marble floors shone like a polished gem under the chandelier. Magnificent artwork graced the walls, and thick Aubusson carpets adorned the floors. The butler took their wraps, and Susannah followed Olivia and Sheldrake into the drawing room to meet their hosts.

Lord Derne was a severe-looking man, tall and dark. His wife was quite pretty with fair hair and a ready smile. Susannah curtsied to them both, glad that her slight bobble in balance was overlooked. Once the introductions were made, Lady Derne escorted her toward Lord Ponsby who had accompanied Winston to the theater.

Lord Ponsby wasted no time in bowing over Susannah's hand. "Miss Lacey, how delightful to see you again."

"You two have already met," Lady Derne said. "Ponsby, do be a dear and introduce Miss Lacey about and see to her enjoyment of the evening."

"Gladly." Lord Ponsby extended his arm. "Shall we meet the rest of guests?"

"I should like that above all things." Susannah turned and her insides shuddered. Winston stood near the fireplace. He looked so handsome in his evening dress that her breath had been quite taken away. With a shaky hand, she accepted Lord Ponsby's arm.

Even though she was across the room, Susannah felt Winston's gaze upon her. She looked at him, but his expression gave away nothing. Yet his stare was intense, and Susannah shivered.

"You are cold." Lord Ponsby's voice intruded. "It is this dreadful weather. I have never known a spring to be so poor. Here, you must come and stand by the fire and your friend, Captain Jeffries."

Oh, no, not by *him*! Susannah forced herself to calmly walk beside Lord Ponsby. She would no doubt see Winston often this Season. She could not cower or run away every time their paths crossed. Besides, he owed her an explanation.

"Captain Jeffries, you know Miss Lacey," Lord Ponsby said.

"Miss Lacey." Winston bowed stiffly.

"Good evening, Captain. Did you make it to your club on time last evening?" At his look of confusion, Susannah could not keep from adding, "You were in such a hurry to leave the theater, I was sure you had an appointment." She tried to keep the hurt and anger out of her voice, but failed.

A flicker of annoyance tugged at Winston's forced smile, but he answered calmly. "We made it in ample time."

Lord Ponsby looked uncomfortable, but he nodded his agreement. An undercurrent of tension circled around them. She decided to soften her tone, for Lord Ponsby's sake. "It was a lovely play. Too bad you missed the second half."

"It could not be helped," Winston said. The tension eased somewhat.

"Not at all," Lord Ponsby agreed.

Susannah was at a loss for words. She glanced at her sister and Sheldrake, who spoke with their hosts. Olivia was animated, and Sheldrake smiled, completely relaxed.

"They look well," Winston said quietly.

"I beg your pardon?" she asked.

"Your sister and Lord Sheldrake. They look happy."

"They are immensely happy."

"Lord Sheldrake is your brother by marriage?" Lord Ponsby interjected, obviously impressed by her connections. "Lord Derne speaks highly of him."

"My sister married Sheldrake two years ago." She glanced at Winston, who shifted from one foot to the other. Susannah met Winston while at Sheldrake Hall when she and Olivia were stranded there from a carriage accident. The almost wistful expression on Winston's face surprised her. He remembered their idyllic meetings.

Lady Derne approached Lord Ponsby to ask for his assistance. Once Lord Ponsby excused himself, Susannah realized an opportunity to talk privately with Winston had presented itself. She nervously stepped closer to the fire, which placed her nearer to Winston. He looked ready to bolt, but for propriety's sake, he could not leave a lady standing alone.

"How have you been?" she asked quietly.

"Well." After some hesitation he added, "And you?" He would not look at her.

"I am fine, but I have been worried about you," she blurted. She waited for his response. When he remained quiet, she asked, "Why did you not write to me? After reading that you fell at Toulouse"—her voice had become thick with emotion, but she forged onward—"I feared the worst."

He met her gaze. She thought she detected some pain there, or perhaps it was merely regret. But then it was gone. "Susannah," he whispered.

She almost melted at the sound of her name on his lips—the sound that had haunted her dreams for years.

"Now is not the time to discuss this, but I must say that I am heartily sorry for causing you distress," he said quietly.

She was rendered speechless. He was merely sorry. The butler announced that dinner was served, and Susannah could have cried with frustration.

Lord Ponsby suddenly appeared at her side, offering his arm to escort her to the dining room. Winston stood rigid with his hands firmly clasped behind his back, his broad shoulders looking that much more impressive. She glanced toward her sister, hoping for a comforting nod, but caught Sheldrake's gaze instead. His frown was deep. No doubt he had witnessed her conversation with Winston.

Lord Ponsby offered his arm to Miss Susannah Lacey. "Shall we proceed to the dining room?"

"Thank you, that would be most agreeable," she answered with hesitation.

Ponsby smiled when she shyly took his arm. She was a lovely young woman whose family had already been approved by his sister and her lofty husband, the Earl of Yarmouth. Miss Lacey's manners were pretty. She lacked the town polish he would need in a wife who would eventually be his countess, but then Miss Lacey had considerable potential.

She also had a connection to Captain Winston Jeffries, one that he suspected could not be easily dismissed, even if that same captain refused to make any claims upon her.

Ponsby made his way to the dining room, introducing Miss Lacey and keeping an interested eye upon her behavior. Yes, he thought, she definitely showed potential.

Winston watched Ponsby escort Susannah as he followed them from a slight distance. The two made a striking pair, both golden haired and elegant. Ponsby laid on the gentlemanly charm, but Winston could not tell whether it was having an effect on Susannah.

It affected him, though. He was still grappling with her sudden appearance and the guilt he felt. He had thought she would have forgotten him, moved on. But seeing her tonight told him otherwise, to his utter shame. Her eyes had betrayed her. In her steady gaze, he saw her anger and hurt and relief all mixed together. She had worried about him, and he had done nothing to prevent her distress.

Seeing her again made him wish he were free to renew their friendship. For the sake of his duty, he had to court Caroline Dunsford. Because of his mission, he could not entertain any soft thoughts where Susannah was concerned. She deserved better than what he was.

They entered the dining room and took their places. Although fourteen sat down to dinner, the atmosphere was informal. The intimate setting promised a free flow of conversation. Ponsby had been correct, it was easier meeting some of society's best in a small dosage.

The first course consisted of turtle soup followed by turbot with lobster sauce. Winston was acutely aware of Susannah, who sat to his left. He noticed her movements as she dipped her spoon into her bowl and then brought it to her lips. Her eyes slanted toward him, and he looked away quickly.

"You are not eating," Susannah whispered.

"I will," he whispered back. He shook out his napkin, careful to keep his left hand low and resting upon his knee. Susannah watched his every move. He saw her eyes widen when she noticed the dreadful scar upon his left hand. She looked ready to ask him about it, but thankfully Ponsby distracted her.

Relieved, Winston turned to the woman on his right who had just asked him about his military status. He danced around the question, answering vaguely that he still had connections.

"So you have sold out?" Susannah asked quietly, entering into the conversation.

"Of course he has," Ponsby answered. "And quite warm, too."

Winston shifted uncomfortably. The plan was to put about gossip that he was deep in funds. He did not expect Ponsby to phrase it straight in front of him.

Winston focused on his plate while the woman to his right spoke across the table to her husband. He scanned the length of the table and connected with a steely gaze that belonged to Lord Sheldrake. Winston nodded politely. Lord Sheldrake tipped his head in acknowledgment, but there was no affability in his gesture.

Winston had paid his respects to Lord Sheldrake and his wife before they sat down to dinner. Lady Sheldrake had received him warmly, but Lord Sheldrake had given him a look of warning that sent a clear message—he would not tolerate any trifling with Susannah. Winston had every intention of heeding Sheldrake's directive. He must stay away from her.

Dinner progressed with each course richer than the last. Finally the dessert ices were served, and soon after, the ladies rose to leave the men to their port. Winston watched Susannah's departure, irritated that he could not keep from staring at her. Her lithe figure was outlined briefly as she walked in front of the fireplace. Winston grabbed a walnut from the bowl and cracked it with a vengeance.

"Delightful young woman," Ponsby said.

Winston knew that he referred to Susannah. "Yes."

"You are not a man of many words are you?"

"Why should I be?" Winston countered.

"I do not know. Perhaps because words are a crucial part of conversation."

Winston merely cocked an eyebrow. "I suppose you have a point there." He took a sip of his port, holding it on his tongue for a moment to savor the strength of it. Leaning back in his chair, Winston listened to the conversation occupying the men at the table. The topic was a popular one, as many of the noblemen present held seats in the House of Lords. They discussed, argued, and contemplated the current economic depression throughout England and what could be done about it. Having no advice to offer, Winston let his thoughts wander toward Susannah. What excuse could he possibly give her for not writing to her?

He supposed he could make something up, but he knew that she would see through any fib that he told. She had always seen through him, or at least she did when they walked together in the fields at Sheldrake Hall. He nearly smiled at the memory floating about in his mind of seeing Susannah for the first time. She had been beautiful then, but she had a youthful innocence that was more ladylike than girlish. She also had poise beyond her tender years and a calm, peaceful spirit that had been balm to his war-torn soul. He knew then that given the chance, he could grow to love her.

The deuce! He wondered if somewhere deep down he may still love her? It did not bear contemplation. He had a mission to complete. He owed her an explanation, and he would give her one. He must tell her that he never felt more than friendship toward her. It was not truly a lie, since three years ago he had assured Lord Sheldrake that his intentions were honorable and only of friendship. His honor forced him to maintain those same intentions.

"Captain Jeffries." Lord Derne's voice interrupted his thoughts. "You have been quiet on this subject. What do you think about the many Englishmen leaving for the Americas?"

Winston came to attention with a blink. He truly hadn't given it a thought at all. Let the bloody chaps go if they wished. All eyes were upon him, and Winston knew that his answer would be severely judged by Ponsby. He must answer correctly. He chose to take a lighter note and said, "If the truth be told, any

Englishman not wishing to live on English soil is an Englishman that England is better off without."

Lord Derne raised his goblet, and the others followed suit with a resounding *here, here*.

Winston relaxed. He had passed his first test with the *ton*.

Susannah let her fingers drift across the keys of the pianoforte. Once Lady Derne found out that Susannah played, she asked her to entertain them. Susannah was grateful to have something to do while the ladies waited for the men to join them. Strains of Beethoven washed over her ears and filled her with a familiar inner peace. Susannah let herself get lost in the music she made. Closing her eyes, she emptied her mind and completely forgot about time.

"A beautiful piece."

Startled, Susannah's eyes flew open to look up at Lord Ponsby. Disappointment filled her. She wished Winston stood before her instead. "Indeed. Are you fond of Beethoven, Lord Ponsby?"

"I cannot say that I am intimately familiar with his music, but I do know enough to identify the talent that you possess."

"Thank you, my lord," she said.

Lord Ponsby rifled through the sheet music until he found what he wanted. "Please play this for me. I can turn the pages for you."

"Of course." Susannah quickly scanned the room. The gentlemen had joined them in full force. Winston stood next to the fireplace, near a group of men gathered there. He conversed easily, yet he remained slightly apart from them, as if he wished to keep his distance.

"Shall we start?" Lord Ponsby had the first page opened and ready for her.

"Yes, of course." Susannah focused her attention upon the sheet music.

"My favorite song," Lord Ponsby said.

Susannah nodded, but she felt annoyed with him and she could not explain why. Lord Ponsby was everything that was gentlemanly. He was also rather dull. She wondered if he tended to be more interested in one's connections or lineage than the real person. Lord Ponsby was not as accepting as Winston. But then, she was comparing him to the Winston she knew three years ago. She did not think Winston was unchanged. In fact, he seemed quite different.

Susannah sighed deeply. Nothing was as it should be. She continued to play until one of the ladies requested a song. Since Susannah had no singing voice, she gave over the pianoforte to a young miss who played as she sang. Lord Ponsby remained to turn the sheet music. Susannah sought out Winston. He sat in a chair near the fireplace and looked half-asleep or bored to tears, she could not tell which.

"Are you enjoying your evening?" she asked as she sat down next to him.

"Yes." His expression was not one of welcome. "I never knew you played so well."

"Thank you," she answered simply.

"Beethoven is my favorite," he whispered. "And quite popular in Prussia."

"He is mine as well. When were you in Prussia?"

"Shhhh," he said. "We must listen."

They could not openly converse while the young lady sang, but even so, Susannah could not pay attention to her. She kept glancing at Winston. She could feel his presence as surely as if he had touched her. The clean scent he wore was faint, but discernible. An ache settled in her chest. He looked completely whole, with no injuries from the war that she could see except for the hideously jagged scar on his left hand.

He caught her looking at it, and Susannah whispered, "Toulouse?"

"No, this happened afterward." He pulled his hand away from her view.

The song ended and the guests politely applauded.

"Winston," she started. "What happened after Toulouse? Why did you not write to me?"

He bowed his head slightly. "Susannah," he said quietly, "I must beg your deepest forgiveness for giving you an incorrect impression. I intended only friendship. If I led you to believe otherwise, I am heartily sorry for it."

Susannah felt his words cut her. Had she misunderstood him all this time? "But the stickpin?" she blurted. "Why would you give me such a thing, if you had no warmth of feeling for me?"

His expression was guarded, his features tight. "Brotherly fondness, I assure you."

"I see." She stood. Winston did as well. "I beg your pardon." She felt like a fool. "I will trouble you no more." She thought she saw a flash of regret in his eyes, but then she could have been mistaken, as she had been when they met. It was three years ago, after all. Perhaps she had built something in her mind and heart that had never been there. "I see my sister and Sheldrake are ready to leave. I am glad to know that you are well, Captain. Do enjoy the Season. I am sure I shall bump into you now and again."

He bowed slightly but said nothing.

*   *   *

Susannah sat cross-legged on the floor by the fire in her bedchamber. Tears streamed down her cheeks, and her hiccups had long since subsided. Winston's letters lay in a bundle in her lap. She had read them over again, and although they were not laced with words of passion, they hinted at something much warmer than mere friendship. She did not understand. Winston had made it quite clear tonight that he wanted nothing to do with her. She should accept that the love she felt for him was not returned. But she did not want to, not after seeing him alive when she feared he was dead.

Wiping her tears away with the back of her hand, she bundled up the letters and rose to her knees. She'd burn them and be done with this obsession of hers. Leaning toward the grate, she held one letter in her hand just over the flames. She pulled her hand back when she heard a knock at the door.

"Yes," she said with a sniff.

Olivia slipped through the door. "May I come in?"

"Of course." Susannah watched her sister walk toward her and sit down in the overstuffed chair near the hearth. "Did you enjoy Lady Derne's dinner party?"

"I did," Olivia said. "They are nice people." Olivia brushed back Susannah's hair before asking, "What are you doing?"

Susannah raised the letters. "I am going to burn them."

"Oh, dearest, what has he done?"

Susannah felt more tears burning for release at the corners of her eyes. She tried to swallow and then burst into tears anew. Her sister knelt down next to her and cradled her in her arms. "I am such a fool," Susannah sobbed.

"What has happened?" Olivia stroked her head.

Susannah sniffled and pushed away from her sister's embrace. "I had believed all these years that Winston loved me. But now, I think I must have been mistaken. Winston apologized for leading me to believe his intentions were more than friendship."

Olivia narrowed her eyes. "I saw the two of you talking, as did Richard. Neither of us wish to see you hurt, Susannah. It was all I could do to keep my husband away from your captain." Olivia looked hesitant, as if she wanted to say something.

"What is it?" Susannah prodded.

Her sister sighed. "I do not believe you were mistaken. I know what I saw three years ago, Susannah, and your Winston had more on his mind than mere friendship."

"Then why does he tell me otherwise?"

"Because things can change over time. Perhaps it is true that your captain does not feel the way he once did." Olivia took a deep breath and let it out before she added, "Or perhaps he thinks he should not care for you."

Susannah grasped the bit of hope Olivia offered. "I see." But still she felt confused.

"May I offer a bit of advice to you, dear?" Olivia asked as she stood. "If you truly love this man, do not give up on him just yet."

"But what of Sheldrake?" Her hope grew and warmed her heart.

"I shall take care of Richard. He only wants to protect you." Olivia caressed Susannah's cheek. "If you love Winston, and if he loves you in return, the hurt you feel along the journey is quite worth the final prize. I married once for the wrong reasons, and you remember where that left me. But now I am married to the love of my life, my soul's mate. Trust me, Susannah, when I say to you, do not settle for anything less." She got up and walked to the door. "Good night, my dear."

Susannah watched her sister leave. Since both her father and mother died soon after Susannah had been born, she looked to Olivia and Aunt Agatha for parental guidance. Susannah trusted her sister's opinion like none other. She sat upon the floor for what seemed like ages. She remembered every look from Winston, every word he had uttered since meeting him at Drury Lane in an attempt to read whatever hidden meanings or feelings might lie beyond them. It was frustrating that she could not tell what he felt toward her. He was different than he had been. There was a secretive intensity in him that she had not remembered.

Olivia was right. She wanted Winston, and she could not give up on him just yet. Not without a fight, at least.

She got to her feet and ran to the opened door of her armoire. The first step was to choose a proper dress for Lady Derne's rout in three days. She ran her fingers over her newly purchased silks and muslins. Her dress would have to be white, since this was her first official outing, but it must also display her figure in a manner to catch Winston's notice.

A thrill of excitement bubbled within her. Her sister had given her hope. If Winston had strong feelings for her once, surely she could make him feel them again. She gathered up his letters and kissed each one. "Winston," she whispered, "will you be mine own?"

Chapter Three

*W*inston's valet brushed his shoulders after helping him into a Weston coat of blue superfine. The man was a former batman in the military who had turned his talents to dressing his betters after the officer he served was killed at Waterloo. Winston turned to face the smaller man. "Pegston, how do I look?"

"Like a lofty cove." Pegston nodded his head in approval.

"Good. That is the appearance I am after." Winston turned back to look into the glass where he preened a bit further. There was evidence of another sleepless night under his eyes, but the smudges were light, so he paid them no heed.

Pegston had noticed as well, but had not fussed over him. Winston was glad for that. No doubt his new valet of two days had heard him tossing about in the middle of the night, but the man had asked no questions. Winston wondered if perhaps it was not unusual for a man home from the wars to have nightmares. Perhaps Pegston had dreams of his own to contend with.

Tonight he would meet Miss Caroline Dunsford at the Derne rout. She was the daughter of Lord Dunsford, his target and suspected Napoleon sympathizer. He had to own that he was nervous, but not due to his expected introduction. He fiddled with his sleeve. His jitters stemmed more from the prospect of seeing Susannah again. He had to act indifferent toward her for the sake of them both. He had a mission to complete. He could afford no distractions.

Winston remembered the look of utter disbelief upon Susannah's face when he had referred to his brotherly feelings for her. He knew it hurt her, but how Susannah reacted to that hurt bothered him. She had controlled her features into such a calm facade that Winston felt lower than a horse's hoof. Her eyes had been stormy with emotion so raw and painful that he had to look away in shame.

He dabbed his fingers into his jar of Marrow Pomade, then lightly combed it through his hair. He needed a haircut, but this would do until he could sit still long enough for Pegston to give him one.

The last two days had been full ones. He had rented a modest town house in an excellent part of Mayfair at a decent price. Lucky for him, the expected tenants had canceled at the last moment. It came with a small staff of servants, including a groom and a fairly well-stocked stable. His newly hired valet had accompanied him to Weston's where Winston purchased a small but excellently made wardrobe. After Ponsby's comments at White's, he made sure that at least two of his coats were of the latest style.

"There," Winston said with a sigh. "This is as good as I can possibly present myself."

"You'll have the ladies begging for your attention, sir."

"I need have only one that begs." Winston needed

Miss Dunsford's attentions in order to gain entry to her home and search through her father's things.

Pegston smirked. "Got yer eye fixed already, have ye?"

"In a matter of speaking, yes." Winston proceeded to place a small beaver upon his head, then he pulled on his gloves. "Thank you, Pegston. Do not wait up."

" 'Course not." The man actually winked.

Winston chuckled as he left his dressing room. He entered the small front parlor, and paced back and forth, waiting for Ponsby.

"Well, well," Ponsby drawled after he arrived. "You have been to Weston's."

"I have." Winston felt irritated by the compliment, almost as if there was a set-down lurking in his tone somewhere.

"Let us leave, then," Ponsby said. "The drive is long."

Winston climbed into Ponsby's well-sprung curricle and relaxed against the supple leather of the seats.

"Your Miss Lacey will be attending tonight's rout," Ponsby said.

"I know."

"A lovely creature."

"She is." Winston didn't much feel like discussing Susannah when he was trying very hard not to think about her.

"I should like to call on her tomorrow. Would you care to join me?" Ponsby asked warily.

Winston knew what he was doing. He wanted Winston's blessing to pay court to Susannah. It was noble of the clod to consider his feelings in the matter. "No." Winston tried for indifference. "You go on ahead, but perhaps you would accompany me when I call upon Miss Dunsford tomorrow afternoon."

Ponsby smiled. "Yes, of course. I had planned on it. It will solidify your place in society to be seen regularly with me." His tone was completely matter-of-fact, so Winston knew it was said without conceit. "Shall we agree upon half past two? Then we can part company, and I shall call upon Miss Lacey."

"Very well."

"It is settled," Ponsby said with a nod.

"Indeed," Winston said. They were silent the rest of the way.

Susannah left her pelisse with the butler when she entered the foyer with her family. Lord and Lady Derne extended a warm greeting of welcome and ushered them into the main hall that was already filled to a sad crush. Susannah swept a quick glance down the front of her gown. The white muslin she chose to wear was similar to the gowns worn by most the young ladies present.

Fortunately, Lady Evelyn had been the one to oversee the choosing of her come-out wardrobe instead of her conservative aunt. Susannah was grateful that the neckline of the evening dress she wore was slightly deeper than many of the other young misses'. Her sufficient bosom was displayed to advantage without appearing immodest.

Susannah breathed deeply and squared her shoulders. She had to find Winston. She would make sure that he saw her often. She had planned her strategy as carefully as she had her appearance. She had to capture Winston's notice as often as possible. Next, she planned to show him that she had grown up and was comfortable moving in these lofty circles. She would talk to him in a harmlessly friendly manner and see what reaction she could detect from him.

"Rather a lot of people, wouldn't you say?" Sheldrake asked to no one in particular.

"I believe they call it a *crush*. It is the desired state for a rout, you know," she said.

Her brother-in-law smiled. "I imagine there are many handsome gentlemen for you to meet."

She did not miss the subtle inquiry in his voice. He was a dear to worry about her. She placed her hand upon his. "Yes, I imagine there are. I shall enjoy myself immensely, you may rest assured."

"Come, let us make the rounds, then," he said.

She took Sheldrake's left arm, and Olivia took his right, and they wove their way through the throng of people, stopping to make conversation where they could.

Despite the crowd, it was not long before Lord Ponsby approached her. "Good evening, Miss Lacey." He bowed before her.

"Good evening, Lord Ponsby. You have met my sister and her husband, have you not?" she asked him.

"Indeed I have." Lord Ponsby extended his hand to Lord Sheldrake.

"Yes, of course." Susannah stood quietly as Lord Ponsby spoke briefly with them. The ballroom had been opened for this evening's rout, and candlelight glimmered from every sconce on every wall. Two exquisite chandeliers hung from the high ceiling, and musicians played softly against the east wall. It was everything a party should be.

"Come." Lord Ponsby offered his arm. "I shall escort you to the refreshment table."

Susannah scanned the room for Winston, but he was not to be found. "Very well, lead on," she said, taking Lord Ponsby's extended arm. They stopped many times, and Lord Ponsby introduced several lords and ladies to Susannah. She hoped she would remember their names the next time she saw them.

It was terribly difficult to appear interested when she cared only about seeing Winston. Finally, she spotted him. He looked incredibly handsome in a deep blue evening coat that hugged his broad shoulders to perfection. He spoke to a rather petite young lady with dark hair piled high upon her head in glossy sausage curls. Unwanted jealousy swamped her.

"Ah, here we are," Lord Ponsby said with a gesture toward the table.

"My goodness, what wonderful choices," she said with a distracted air.

"These sandwiches are wonderful. Would you care for one?" Lord Ponsby asked.

She shook her head. "I thank you, but no." Many of the foods were things she had never tried nor seen before. As Lord Ponsby filled a small plate for himself, Susannah kept declining the delicacies he offered while watching Winston and the little dark-haired lady. "I shall simply have a piece of that cake and some punch."

Lord Ponsby nodded and handed her a plate of cake.

Susannah stood staring at Winston as he smiled and nodded and chatted with the petite miss who looked far too young to be out. She stuffed the cake into her mouth and swallowed without tasting it. She had to move quickly.

"Your punch," Lord Ponsby offered.

She drank the contents nearly in one gulp. "Come." Susannah set the dishes down upon the table with a clink. "I see Captain Jeffries, let us go and say good evening to him."

"Very well." Lord Ponsby begrudgingly left his own half full plate of food on the table and offered his arm.

Susannah felt a prick of conscience, but confronting Winston was surely more important than food.

Over and over Susannah tried to recall what she had planned to say to Winston, but her mind had gone completely blank. All she could see was Winston making moon faces over a tiny girl dressed in pale pink. Susannah decided then and there that she hated pink.

"Good evening, Captain Jeffries," Susannah said too loudly when she stood before him.

He nearly jumped. "Miss Lacey, and Ponsby, how nice to see you both."

Lord Ponsby bowed to Miss Petite Pink. "Miss Dunsford, I'd like to introduce to you, Miss Susannah Lacey."

"How do you do." Miss Dunsford curtsied beautifully.

"Very well, I thank you." Susannah returned the curtsy, but it was nowhere near as graceful. A terrible desire to knock the young lady down took hold of Susannah.

The four of them stood close together as the swell of the crowd pushed into the room. A gentleman bumped into Susannah, which caused her to trip into Winston's arm. He reached out and grabbed hold of her elbow to steady her. He let go of her just as quickly.

"I beg your pardon," she whispered.

"Not at all." Winston's expression was unreadable.

Susannah glanced at Lord Ponsby, who chatted with Miss Dunsford and another young miss who had joined in their conversation. Susannah turned her back on them so that she could stand directly in front of Winston. "You look well this evening," she said.

"As do you." She did not mistake the brief look he gave to her bodice, and her heart sang a small victory song. He was not indifferent toward her physically, at least that was a start. She stepped an inch closer to him.

"You changed your hair," he said finally and stepped back.

"Do you like it?" She stepped forward and smiled.

His eyes flashed a look of what she hoped was desire. "I do," he said.

"Thank you." She did not know what else to say, and an awkward silence settled over them. She lost her nerve and retreated a step backward just as Lord Ponsby intruded.

"Miss Turnbridge, this is Captain Jeffries and Miss Lacey." Lord Ponsby introduced the young lady they had been speaking with at length.

Susannah nodded to them both. Winston bowed over Miss Turnbridge's hand.

"I was just telling Miss Dunsford and Miss Turnbridge about your shining military career," Lord Ponsby said. "And they are simply dying for a story."

Susannah looked at Winston. His face had gone a shade lighter. She wondered why such a question would make him uncomfortable.

"Captain Jeffries," Miss Dunsford said. "Pray, what regiment did you captain?"

"The Second Queen's Dragoon Guard," Winston answered slowly. He hoped that Susannah would not ask him what had happened to him after Toulouse. He was not up to a scene.

"How wonderful," Miss Turnbridge squeaked. "A cavalry man."

Winston glanced at Miss Dunsford, who eagerly awaited his story. She could be considered a lovely young lady if one appreciated fragile beauty. "Yes, er, well," Winston stammered.

"Captain Jeffries," Miss Turnbridge said shyly. "Was it very terrible fighting the French?"

Winston nearly rolled his eyes in frustration. Did the chit think it had been a grand picnic? "Yes, Miss Turnbridge it was a terrible thing. But many of the French were honorable chaps just following commands."

"As you had to?" Susannah asked.

"Yes," he answered.

"Come, now, Captain. Do tell us a story, Lord Ponsby said that you were highly commended," Miss Dunsford urged.

Miss Turnbridge looked on as if she could hardly stand still with waiting for him to speak. Susannah watched him closely. Too closely. He wondered if she sensed his discomfort at being the center of attention. But he had to play the gallant suitor to Miss Dunsford. Perhaps a heroic war story was just the thing to impress her.

He cleared his throat. "I was in Spain with Wellington's army at Salamanca. It was terribly hot. French troops flooded the area, but even so, Wellington staged a brilliant attack. The British cavalries formed across from the French cavalry called the cuirassiers. We faced each other proudly that day. But the English wanted the win more. We wanted a victory so badly that we could smell it. We charged and engaged the cuirassiers while the infantry followed to finish the fighting on foot. We took that battle and won, but there were many casualties."

"When was that?" Susannah asked.

"About a year before we met." Winston sought her

gaze and nearly kicked himself for his error when he saw the satisfaction in her eyes.

"You have met Miss Lacey before this Season?" Miss Turnbridge asked.

Winston noticed that Miss Dunsford did not look pleased. Perhaps she was jealous of Susannah. If so, it was a good sign. He thought carefully before he answered. "Yes. Miss Lacey and I are old *friends*. I spent some time during the summer a couple years ago near her brother-in-law's estate, Sheldrake Hall." He hoped that he sounded convincing enough that they were family friends.

Miss Dunsford's frown cleared slightly. "Oh, I see." She turned to Miss Turnbridge. "They are old friends."

Miss Turnbridge smiled at Winston then at Susannah. "How delightful."

He noticed Susannah's raised eyebrow and the defiant look in her eye. Obviously, she did not believe him the other night when he had apologized for misleading her. He simply had to work harder in order to convince her. He needed to redirect what he felt for Susannah toward Miss Dunsford. He had to focus on her, the target of his mission.

"You are a very brave man," Miss Dunsford announced.

"I did my duty only," he said. His modesty earned him a smile from Miss Dunsford and a frown from Susannah.

"Fortunately for you ladies, our fine Captain Jeffries no longer needs face the danger of war. Instead, he faces the formidable *ton* matrons," Ponsby said to the titters of Miss Turnbridge.

Winston could have kicked him. It was hardly a

subtle announcement of his pretend search for a bride.

"It must have been truly frightening, not knowing when one might fall. And you did fall, did you not at Toulouse?" Susannah asked innocently.

She knew that he had. Perhaps she was punishing him for the wrong he did her. It was her due, he supposed, but he was not about to explain everything here, and so he hesitated in his answer.

"Do not say that you were injured? My goodness, where?" Miss Dunsford asked.

Winston cast an irritated glance at Susannah, who merely smiled calmly in return. "A saber wound straight through me." He gestured toward his side. "Here."

"How dreadful," Miss Dunsford said with real distaste.

"Truly," Ponsby agreed.

"Let us talk of something more pleasant," Winston said. He had effectively shocked them into letting the matter drop. With a wink of his eye, he asked. "What is the next event for you ladies?"

Miss Turnbridge giggled, and Miss Dunsford smiled at him. He was making progress, but flirtation was difficult work! Perhaps it was because his attentions to the lady were only in hope of spying on her father.

"Almack's will be opening their rooms this coming Wednesday," Miss Dunsford said.

"Very good, I do hope you shall save me a dance," Winston said to Miss Dunsford. When she hesitated, he realized the tactical error he had made in singling her out. "All of you must save a dance for me," he added.

Miss Turnbridge colored slightly and giggled her agreement that she would.

"I shall look forward to a waltz," Susannah whispered for his ears alone.

A fleeting shot of desire ripped through him when he thought of holding her in his arms. If he had any sense, he would resist the temptation to waltz with Susannah. He needed to distance himself from her. He was all too aware of her standing quietly beside him. Her perfume was soft, and her gown draped her form too nicely. His duty required that he succeed in courting Miss Dunsford. Any desire he felt for Susannah must be focused toward Miss Dunsford. He would hurt Susannah, but then she would be better off without him. He looked regretfully at Miss Dunsford. He must use her, an innocent bystander, to get to her father. He was more determined than ever to quit the spying business once he saw this mission done.

"Miss Dunsford, Miss Turnbridge, would you care to make our way to the refreshments? I know Lord Ponsby wanted to show Miss Lacey the lovely balcony." He cast a pointed look at Ponsby.

Ponsby was not a dull-wit. He smiled and offered his arm to a disappointed Susannah. She could do nothing but follow him.

"We should like that above all things, Captain Jeffries," Miss Dunsford agreed.

He offered each lady his arm, and to the food table they went. He had to own that he was in sore need of refreshment. Once he had plied each lady with food and punch, Winston relaxed and chatted amiably with the two ladies until they excused themselves to mingle. Despite his modest success with Miss Dunsford, he knew he had a long way yet to go. She was rather a cool young lady.

Standing in front of the refreshment table, sipping the punch, Winston watched Susannah in the distance. Ponsby introduced her to numerous people, and she charmed them all with her ready smile. She moved easily among this group of the upper ten thousand, as if she had been born to it. It was the world she had dreamed of entering when they first met. He remembered the longing in her voice when she spoke of having a Season but had been shy of the funds to realize her wish. With Sheldrake as her guardian, those funds had become ample and readily available to her. No doubt her dowry was substantial. She would not lack for suitors this season.

Winston swallowed the last of his punch with feelings of regret swirling around in the pit of his stomach. If only things had been different. If he had remained the same man that he once was, perhaps he could have pursued Susannah. He cursed silently for allowing his attraction to show. Yet, she seemed to bait him into it. He wondered if perhaps she was planning revenge on him somehow. He had hurt her.

Even so, there could be no future for them. She'd eventually want no part of a husband who lacked the funds to support her in the style she had grown accustomed to. She would not relish the idea of sleeping next to a man who suffered from violent nightmares. Winston took another sip of punch. The deuce! He sometimes wondered if he'd eventually lose his sanity from the lack of a restful night.

Perhaps he should encourage Ponsby. In no time Susannah would see him as the better man. The more he learned of Ponsby's character, the more he liked him. He was a bit arrogant, Winston supposed, but then the man had considerable wealth and a lofty title to inherit. Ponsby had an agreeable family that would no doubt welcome Susannah warmly. Susannah was better off with Ponsby. It was plain to see.

Caroline Dunsford did not know what to think of the latest beauty to make her come-out. Miss Susannah Lacey had an angelic face and eyes of sky-blue, and her family connections must be highly respectable in order to have Lord Ponsby take notice of her.

Caroline narrowed her gaze as she watched her new rival move about the ballroom. It was well-known that Lord Ponsby wanted to set up his nursery. He had been on the Marriage Mart the last two years. This Season he returned to it yet again. "Just like I have," Caroline whispered bitterly.

Last year she made her come-out in the hopes of finding a love match. Above all things, she longed for a gentleman who would offer her true love and security. Every man who had courted her last year was a clinging, overly forward, grasping fortune hunter. She found the whole Season distasteful, and yet here she was again, hoping to catch Lord Ponsby's attention, and he did not even know that she existed.

Lord Ponsby had been the only gentleman who had treated her as a real person, not simply a pretty face with a whopping-sized dowry attached. She felt comfortable in his presence. She wished to deepen their relationship, but he had kept his distance from her. And now this Season, he showed a marked interest in the golden Miss Lacey while she had been left behind with an edgy army captain.

She sipped her punch and considered her options. Perhaps, the courtship of this captain was just what she needed. He was Lord Ponsby's friend, after all. If she encouraged the captain, would the lord eventually follow? It was worth a try, but she needed to tread carefully. She should not be too accepting toward this Captain Jeffries. Although his flirtation was awkward, she did not think him shy. The man had a raw power in him that she found quite unsettling. He appeared to care no more for polite society than the man in the moon. He was not for her. She was determined to have Lord Ponsby. He was the man she must catch this Season.

Chapter Four

*W*inston welcomed Ponsby into his small drawing room. Ponsby arrived an hour before they planned to call upon Miss Dunsford at her home. It would be Winston's first chance to search for the traitorous letter he sought. "Would you care for some brandy?" he asked.

"Before calling upon a lady?" Ponsby looked shocked.

"Tea then," Winston amended. He actually enjoyed causing the overly proper Ponsby a bit of distress. He rang for tea and offered his guest a seat. Winston remained standing by the fireplace. He swore he would never get used to the damp chill that was England. This spring was colder than most he remembered. "What brings you here so early?"

"I shall not beat about the bush, I have a proposition for you."

"Do you?" Winston stoked up the fire with the iron before taking a seat across from Ponsby. "Well, then, let me hear it."

Ponsby shifted in his seat. "I do not wish you to take this the wrong way. We have known each other only briefly, yet I believe you are a man of your word, and Lord Castlereagh says you are someone to be trusted. In fact, he told me you had requested a post in India once you were finished here."

"Now I am truly curious," Winston interrupted as he leaned forward to rest his elbows upon his knees.

"I am considering a business venture in India and I need a partner."

Winston breathed deeply in an attempt to contain his excitement. Ponsby could not know how much he wanted the chance to make his fortune in India. "I see" was all he could manage.

"I will understand if you feel that entering in trade is something you would prefer not to do, but I can assure you as a gentleman, the opportunity for eventual gain is quite promising."

Winston leaned back in his chair. "What is it that you would have me do?"

"I wish to purchase a company that manufactures spices for export all over the world, but I will need a man there that I can trust to oversee the operation," Ponsby explained.

"And what if I receive the military post in India as I have requested?"

"I am sure that we might work around your military schedule. I cannot promise much of an income at first. But later on, if you choose to sell out your commission entirely, I believe this venture will be worthwhile for you. You may choose either way. The company is running at a deficit currently, since the owner has bled the very life out of it. I need a good man on-site to turn the profits around. It could take a few years, but I am confident of success eventually. I have a head for these things. This is my way of making additional income so that I need not rely solely upon my father."

"I see." Winston tried to digest this excellent piece of news. It surprised him to learn that Ponsby dabbled in business. It proved that he was neither spoiled nor idle. "What investment would you require from me to enter such a partnership?" He mentally made note of the modest balance of his account in the Bank of England.

"Time, my dear captain. What I require is an agreed amount of time spent in India until the business is stable and profitable. That would be your investment. The profits can be split between us sixty-forty, forty percent to you and sixty percent to me. I wish to be the owning shareholder, but you shall have considerable freedom to make decisions even so."

"Of course," Winston said. It was a generous offer. If he chose to, he could one day return to England a rich nabob. He saw no reason whatsoever for refusing. Destiny, it seemed, had finally paid him a visit.

"You will want to think on it, I am sure," Ponsby said.

The housekeeper arrived with tea, and she proceeded to pour a dish for each man. Winston took a warm scone and popped half of it into his mouth. He knew he did not need to think on it. It was the opportunity of a lifetime.

He thought of Susannah. By accepting Ponsby's offer, he promised to be gone from England for a very long while. Perhaps that was just as well, since he did not wish to witness Susannah wed. If she chose Ponsby, he would still be miles away.

Once the housekeeper left the parlor, Winston stood. Brushing the crumbs from his fingers, he offered his hand to Ponsby. "I am quite sure that I needn't think on it long. I accept your offer Ponsby. In fact, I am heartily looking forward to it."

Ponsby took his hand and shook it three times before letting go. "I will have my solicitors draw up the papers, and we can discuss the matter further. We can settle upon the amount of time you will need to reside there once the papers are ready."

"I give you my word as a gentleman," Winston said. "I will do what it takes, for as long as it takes, to make our company successful."

Ponsby smiled as he took a scone. Then with a look of merriment in his eye, he said, "I may make a rich gentleman out of you yet."

Winston grinned in return and with good-natured sarcasm, he responded, "Why Ponsby, I don't quite know what to say."

Ponsby burst out laughing.

Winston slapped Ponsby on the back. "Come on, let's take your gig to call upon Miss Dunsford. Mine is having a wheel repaired."

Susannah peered out of the window. They were late. She paced the drawing room floor, much to her aunt's disapproval. Lord Ponsby had called on her earlier in the afternoon to invite her for a drive in Hyde Park. She had hesitated until he informed her that Winston and Miss Dunsford would be joining them. And now she was having second thoughts.

It was one thing to chase Winston when it was merely the two of them. It was another thing entirely to be forward when others were nearby to witness it. The problem was Miss Dunsford. Winston appeared interested in her and she in him. How on earth was she to compete against the tiny Miss Pink and Perfect?

"Wearing a path in the carpet will not bring them here any sooner," Aunt Agatha said.

"Yes, dear. You should sit demurely so that you

make a pretty picture for the gentlemen when they arrive. I hear a carriage even now," Lady Evelyn added.

Susannah dashed to the window overlooking Grosvenor Square. The carriage did indeed stop in front of their town house. She watched as Lord Ponsby and Winston got out and headed for the door. She tried to hurry across the room to sit down, but she caught the toe of her slipper in the hem of her carriage dress. She fell down to her knees with a gasp.

"Oh, my dear, are you all right?" Lady Evelyn asked.

Winston, who stood at the entrance of the room, rushed to her side before the housekeeper could even announce them. "Are you hurt?" he asked with concern.

"No. I am just fine." Susannah felt more embarrassed than anything. She placed her hand in Winston's palm and glanced up at his face. She noticed the corners of his mouth twitched. She could have crawled beneath the carpet and stayed there.

"You will have to watch where you step," he whispered as he helped her to her feet.

"No doubt," she said. She brushed out her gown and noticed that no damage had been done. It had taken her far too long to choose this primrose yellow with its matching spencer and bonnet.

"Lord Ponsby and Captain Jeffries," the housekeeper belatedly announced.

Susannah rolled her eyes in frustration. Lord Ponsby stood in the doorway, looking completely uncertain, and Winston still had a hold of her hand. His earlier expression of amusement was replaced with warmth. She could have melted. But then his eyes turned guarded, as if a door into his heart had been closed from her. He let go of her hand that instant.

"Ah, Lord Ponsby, Captain Jeffries." Lady Evelyn glided toward them with her hands outstretched. "So nice to see you both again." Lady Evelyn turned to Winston. "You remember Miss Wilts, do you not, Captain?"

"Yes, of course I do," Winston bowed.

Susannah did not wish to dawdle. "I believe it is getting late, and we still have Miss Dunsford to pick up, is that so?"

"It is," Lord Ponsby said.

"Very well," Susannah said. "I shall return well before dinner."

"I will see to it that she is not late," Lord Ponsby added.

Once outside, Susannah noticed the elegant crested barouche that could only belong to Lord Ponsby. "A fine carriage," she said. Sheldrake's groomsman held the ribbons, while Lord Ponsby helped her into her seat.

Winston hopped up unto the rear-facing seat.

In no time they had taken the three blocks to the Dunsford estate on Piccadilly near Green Park. Susannah remained seated next to Lord Ponsby, and Winston went inside to fetch Miss Dunsford.

"Are you enjoying the Season?" Lord Ponsby asked when they were alone.

"I am." Her gaze stayed riveted upon the front door of Dunsford House.

"Your first one, is it not?"

"It is." Susannah kept glancing at the front door. What on earth was keeping the two of them? She ventured to guess that Miss Diminutive Pink Dunsford was not ready. Winston was no doubt kept cooling his heels in the drawing room.

Tired of looking at a closed door, Susannah turned to face Lord Ponsby. "My lord, how long have you known Winston, I mean, Captain Jeffries?"

"Not long. We met that evening at the theater."

"I see." She fiddled with the edge of her pelisse. "You have hit it off rather well it appears." She had taken them for very good friends.

"He is a good chap." Lord Ponsby twisted the reins around his hand, and then untwisted them. The horses stamped their feet, as if sensing their master's impatience to be gone.

"He is a childhood friend of mine, you know," Susannah said as she watched the door. Finally they came out.

"Who's that?" This time it appeared that Lord Ponsby was barely listening.

"Captain Jeffries," Susannah said.

"What about me?" Winston asked. He and Miss Dunsford had appeared beside the carriage. Miss Dunsford was dressed in pink once again, only this time it was a deeper shade of rose. Susannah had to admit the color did look well on her.

"I was simply explaining to Lord Ponsby," Susannah said, "that you and I are childhood friends. Miss Dunsford, how very nice to see you, again." She hoped that her greeting to Miss Pink sounded convincingly polite. Her smile felt broad enough almost to the point of pain.

Winston narrowed his gaze as he looked at Susannah; now what was she up to? "Yes, of course," he said as he helped Miss Dunsford into the carriage.

"Good afternoon, Miss Lacey," Miss Dunsford said coolly. She quickly looked at Lord Ponsby. "And my lord, how good to see you again."

"Miss Dunsford." Ponsby nodded. "There, I believe we are ready to go." He clicked the reins, and the horses pulled away from the curb. They headed toward Hyde Park at a spanking pace.

Winston settled back to enjoy the ride. Mayfair in the April sunshine was a beautiful place, and today the weather had cooperated. It was seasonally warm. Since Ponsby and Susannah sat with their backs to them, he had trouble hearing their conversation, but then considering how fast Ponsby drove, Winston imagined they could not speak much. It would take all of Ponsby's concentration not to overturn the carriage, Winston thought sourly. What was it about titled gentlemen that they must live dangerously through their driving skills?

"Lord Ponsby's quite a whip, is he not?" Miss Dunsford asked with exhilaration.

"If you consider speed a prerequisite, why then, yes, he is," Winston replied. He was immediately sorry for his sarcastic tone, since Miss Dunsford raised a delicate dark brow. He decided that he must flirt to make up for his comment. Leaning closer, he asked, "Do you like to go fast, Miss Dunsford?"

Shock registered on her face, but she smiled demurely. "I do not mind speed in a carriage."

He cursed himself silently. That came out completely wrong. He had come on too strong and insulted the very proper and cool Miss Dunsford. It did not help matters that while he tried to woo his target, Susannah sat just behind him, her back nearly touching his own. Her floral scent kept tickling his nose, and the ribbons to her bonnet flew backward in the wind to brush his neck. He flicked them aside and turned to better face Miss Dunsford. It was proving difficult to bury the attraction he had for Susannah and concentrate on Miss Dunsford. He was battle tested for pity's sake. But this kind of warfare was waged in the heart, and he feared which side he was on. It did not help matters that Susannah was right there on the battlefield. He felt deuced uncomfortable trying to flirt with Miss Dunsford when Susannah sat within earshot, but he had to give it another go. "Is this your first Season?" he asked.

"No, it is my second."

"Oh." His mind searched for the right words. "Such a beauty as you," he purred. Yes, that was good, he thought. "I am surprised that you were not snatched up by a handsome gallant."

This earned him a slight blush of the cheek. "Really, Captain Jeffries, you are too kind. I simply did not find someone who would suit."

"I see. Perhaps this year shall be different," he said.

She smiled and added, "I do hope so."

Ponsby slowed the carriage as they entered Hyde Park. The traveling paths were littered with carriages and phaetons of society folk intending to be seen rather than to enjoy the park's beauty. Winston smirked as he considered the scene before him. He'd never make a town dandy, of that he was certain. He did not give a hang what these arbiters of fashion thought of him, and yet, he had to play the pretty to impress Miss Dunsford. And she proved that she was not impressed easily. Miss Dunsford nearly looked down her nose at his efforts to flirt with her. He had to do better.

He turned to look at Susannah, who sat up straight in her seat, her eyes wide, as Ponsby pointed out the highest sticklers of society. Something in her demeanor struck a chord within him. Susannah looked a bit overwhelmed by the lesson of who was who in

London. He found himself wondering if Susannah would be happy as Ponsby's future countess. Much would be expected of her. He shook his doubts away. Ponsby was a good man with everything to offer Susannah. Winston had a past and an undetermined future. There was no comparison.

They joined the line of conveyances traveling around the track. Several carriages stopped so that the occupants could chitchat with those in the carriages moving opposite. They were at a standstill. Miss Dunsford looked bored, and Winston was at a loss to rouse her interest.

Lord Ponsby swung around in his seat and asked, "How are you both back there?"

Winston watched in amazement as Miss Dunsford lit up like a firefly when she smiled at Ponsby. He observed the way a blush stole into her cheeks as she spoke to him, and Winston knew he was thoroughly sunk! How could he succeed in wooing Miss Dunsford if she desired Lord Ponsby? "This is just fine," he muttered.

"I think that it would be more enjoyable to get out and walk," Susannah said.

"Is that agreeable to you?" Ponsby asked.

"I should like that above all things," Miss Dunsford answered before Winston had a chance to say anything on the matter.

Ponsby clicked the reins, and the horses slowly pulled the carriage out of line and down the wide path to where several others had been parked before an expanse of lush green grass. Winston hopped out of the barouche once it had stopped. He turned to help Miss Dunsford, but to his surprise, Ponsby had beaten him to it. Ponsby helped Miss Dunsford, then proceeded to escort her to where he tethered the horses.

He looked quickly at Susannah to gauge her reaction to this, but she did not seem to care a whit. She waited for his aide.

A rush of longing skittered through him as he reluctantly reached up to her. Instead of taking his outstretched hand, Susannah nearly fell at him. She placed her hands upon his shoulders. There was nothing for him to do but grab her waist to steady her.

"Thank you," she murmured softly as she practically slid down him. "Does this bring back any memories?"

Winston merely stared at her. His thoughts were indeed thrown back to their walks in the fields behind Sheldrake Hall. But he had not trembled at her touch then as he did now. She had never been so enticingly physical. He needed to retreat fast. He practically jumped away from her.

She swatted him playfully when he did not answer. "I daresay, Winston, the war must have addled your memory. I practically grew up with you as my dearest friend."

Winston coughed to keep from correcting her. They had only spent half of an hour four days in a row at Sheldrake Hall. She made it sound like they had been neighbors. He did not wish to make a scene. Ponsby and Miss Dunsford joined them. "Ah, I remember now," he said.

"How nice to find a dear friend in London," Miss Dunsford said. She turned to Ponsby. "Tell me, where did you purchase such a lovely pair of greys?"

Winston could have groaned with frustration. Miss Dunsford engaged Ponsby in a conversation, and the two drifted ahead of them as they discussed the horses. That left him to entertain Susannah.

Susannah noticed the dismay in Winston's eyes as

he watched Miss Dunsford and Lord Ponsby. Her chance to divert his attention had come. She had been running her latest plan around in her mind the entire drive. She decided that since Winston had claimed only friendship between them, she would indeed be his dear friend, and use that as a reason to be close to him.

Sitting in the front seat next to Lord Ponsby, she had overheard Winston's attempts to flirt with Miss Pink and Pretty Dunsford, and it nearly drove her mad. She wondered what she could possibly do to attract Winston's attention. Her only course of action was to place herself straight under his nose.

Susannah could not claim Winston's interest. In fact, he seemed more annoyed with her. But more than once she thought she saw Winston looking at her with a mixture of longing and regret and Susannah knew the wisdom of her sisters' words. She refused to settle for anything less than Winston's love. "Come." She looped her arm through Winston's. "Let us walk."

Hyde Park was a beautiful expanse of green lawns and ancient oak trees. The Serpentine River lay not far off, and several ladies with their parasols drawn strolled along its sun-washed bank.

He gently pulled free of her and clasped his hands firmly behind his back. "Let us catch up to Ponsby and Miss Dunsford."

She nearly made a face. "They are not far off. Besides, Lord Ponsby is explaining something to her. I think he likes to do that, explain, I mean."

Winston looked sharply at her. "Lord Ponsby is a good man, Susannah. A man that would do well by you if you let him."

Susannah bit her lip, but she did not answer him. She remained quiet as they walked toward the river's edge. Miss Dunsford chatted easily with Lord Ponsby, and Susannah almost envied the ease the two seemed to have with one another. The tension she felt just walking next to Winston was enough to give her a headache. After minutes of painful silence, Susannah asked quietly, "Why did you not write to me and tell me you were alive?"

He sighed. "I told you." He stopped walking to look at her. "I never meant for you to believe that I offered more than my friendship."

Three years ago his gaze spoke of much deeper feelings, as did the tone of his letters that followed. He had to feel more. "But even friends keep in touch," she said.

"I thought it better not to." He would not look at her.

"Better for whom?" she asked.

"For both of us."

"Did you return to your regiment after Toulouse?"

"No."

"But you went back to the fighting." She was trying to understand him.

"In a manner of speaking, yes." He still would not look at her. He dug at the ground with the toe of his fine Hessians. His valet would have a difficult task making the leather shine again. "Come we are falling behind."

Susannah fell silent, but her curiosity was fairly screaming with questions inside her head. What had happened to him after Toulouse? She had heard that a serious injury sometimes changed men. Was that what had happened to Winston?

"A beautiful day for a walk is it not?" Lord Ponsby said when they caught up.

"It is." A dull worry for Winston filled Susannah. Something had happened. She did not think he was the kind of man to disregard his *friends*. Had he not told her when they had met, that he was spending his furlough visiting his lieutenant who lay injured in his home near Sheldrake Hall? That spoke of the kind of friend Winston could be.

"Miss Dunsford," Winston said. "Do you like to skip stones?"

"Why, Captain Jeffries, I have never tried."

Winston grinned with boyish abandon. "Why then, I believe the four of us shall have to enter a challenge. Ponsby, you and Miss Lacey shall be a team. Miss Dunsford and I shall challenge you to a stone-skipping competition."

"What a wonderful idea. I shall try very hard to trounce you, Lord Ponsby," Miss Dunsford said.

Susannah saw admiration shining from Miss Dunsford's eyes, and it suddenly dawned on her that Miss Dunsford had a *tendre* for Lord Ponsby. Relief filled her. Perhaps Miss Dunsford did not have designs upon Winston after all. Susannah felt almost giddy with the realization. Susannah did not want Lord Ponsby even if he might want her. She wanted Winston, who wanted Miss Dunsford but Miss Dunsford wanted Lord Ponsby. The situation was almost humorous. Susannah believed this development might help her plan to capture Winston's heart, if she could use it to her advantage.

"Then, what are we waiting for?" Susannah asked as she took Lord Ponsby by the hand. "Come, let us show the captain and Miss Dunsford how it is done."

"I have never been much of a rock skipper," Lord Ponsby admitted.

But it did not matter as they rushed to the river's edge to find flat smooth stones like a group of children. She was happy to see that even Winston smiled.

"This is what you are looking for Miss Dunsford," Winston said as he held up a perfectly rounded and very flat stone that was about the size of one's palm.

"Oh, but that is far too round, Captain," Susannah corrected him. "I prefer a flat rock with a bit of a pointed edge, in order to keep a better grasp." Susannah approached Miss Dunsford, who picked her way delicately through the stones. "See?" Susannah held out her stone for Miss Dunsford to inspect.

"You appear to be quite the outdoors woman, Miss Lacey," Miss Dunsford said.

Susannah could not tell if Miss Dunsford meant her comment as a compliment. Susannah looked at the dirt on her fingers and considered that perhaps she was not acting like the society miss she tried so hard to be. Susannah wondered if the fascination Winston had for Miss Dunsford was that she was polished and graceful and soft-spoken. She was everything that was London society all rolled into a delicate little body. "Yes, well, I did grow up in the country after all," Susannah muttered softly.

"How delightful for you," Miss Dunsford said sincerely.

Susannah did not understand what Miss Pink and Tiny meant by that statement. She watched Miss Dunsford take two small stones out of Winston's cupped hands. Then she brought them to Susannah for her inspection.

"I have only been used to town living, since my father's estate is here," Miss Dunsford said. "He is very active in politics, however. I have had the good fortune to travel with him, especially after my mother died."

"Oh." Susannah thought that she heard a trace of loneliness in Miss Dunsford's voice, and she felt in charity with her. Susannah had lost her mother at birth. She never had the opportunity to know her. She traded one of Miss Dunsford's stones with one of her own. "That should work better for you. Have you visited many places?"

"My, yes." Her voice took on a dreamier note. "I have been to Italy, Russia, and even Spain."

Susannah glanced at Winston. He had walked away from them to the shore. He stooped down to pick up more stones. Perhaps that was another reason for him to find Miss Dunsford intriguing. Winston once told her that he longed to travel.

She looked Miss Dunsford directly in the eye and responded with complete honesty. "I have always thought that there cannot be a better place than England. I suppose I do not have wanderlust. I am too content to stay here, where I know what to expect."

"Oh, but, Miss Lacey, you truly cannot know until you have seen other places," Miss Dunsford said with conviction. "Travel can be such an adventure."

"I suppose," Susannah murmured.

Winston approached with Lord Ponsby. Each had a handful of stones. She wondered if Winston had overheard their conversation. If she were to marry Winston, would he be content to live in England? She hoped so. Everything she loved was in England—her family and friends. She would not dream of leaving.

"I believe I have quite a few here," Lord Ponsby said with his hands cupped to hold the stones.

Susannah peeked into Lord Ponsby's hands and smiled. "These will do nicely."

Winston grinned. "Ah, but Miss Dunsford and I have the advantage. I am an expert rock skipper."

"You think you are that good do you?" Susannah taunted him.

"I am. It is a basic fact."

"We shall see." Susannah grabbed a couple of stones from Lord Ponsby. "Come, let us have a round of practice first."

They lined up along the river's shore. The sound of water gently lapping along the rocks filled her ears as she watched Winston demonstrate how it was done. He explained gently to Miss Dunsford how to hold the stone between one's fingers and flick with the wrist. She tried a couple of stones, unsuccessfully, which brought Winston to demonstrate with his arms about hers. Susannah's heart sank to the soles of her slippers.

"Here, Lord Ponsby," Susannah whispered. She was bent on beating Miss Dunsford at something. "Give a good throw and see what you can do."

"Miss Lacey, I am not very adept at this." He pulled back his arm and cast the stone. It skittered across the calm water of the river for a total of four skips.

She patted him on the back. "Lord Ponsby, you are very good indeed."

"Thank you, Miss Lacey," he said with satisfaction. "It is your turn, I believe."

Susannah took one of her stones and prepared to throw it. She looked over to where Winston was preparing to throw one of his own. "Shall we commence?" she asked.

"If you wish, but you have not had a practice throw." The breeze ruffled Winston's hair, and his cravat had been loosened slightly. Susannah thought he could not possibly look more handsome.

"I do not believe that I need one, thank you." Susannah leaned back into her throw and then cast it strongly where it skipped five times along the water.

Winston whistled.

"Good show." Lord Ponsby praised her. "You are quite skilled."

They went on this way for nearly half of an hour until, finally Lord Ponsby and Susannah finished as the victors.

Winston came up to them with his hand offered. "May I congratulate you on your victory."

Susannah took his hand for a firm handshake, dirty fingers and all. "I do not plan to lose, Winston, ever," she whispered. She kept hold of his hand a moment longer than necessary so that he would understand her meaning. He did. His eyes darkened to a stormy blue filled with something very close to desire. She smiled at him fully. It was only a matter of time before she captured his heart.

He turned away from her and said, "Let us proceed to Miss Dunsford's home, where we may drown our sorrows in tea." He held out his arm to Miss Dunsford, who took it gingerly, her expression one of mock sorrow for having lost.

Chapter Five

*W*inston stood near the fireplace inside of the Dunsford drawing room and let the heat warm him. Lord Ponsby, Susannah, and Miss Dunsford discussed the successes and failures of their rock-skipping challenge. Winston added his own comments here and again, but his thoughts focused primarily on Susannah. What was he going to do with her?

Susannah had pretty much stated that she was not going to let him go without a fight. But she would have to. He had accepted Ponsby's business proposition. He also had a military post promised to him upon the completion of his mission. Both opportunities took him to India. Susannah did not belong there or anywhere outside of her beloved England, for that matter. She had admitted as much to Miss Dunsford.

If he did not distance himself from Susannah Lacey, she could spell disaster for his future by keeping him in England, where he had no prospects. Winston believed it was better to nurse bruised hearts now rather than later in life after it was too late. He'd seen resentment between couples in his own brother's marriage. He swore he'd never experience it. Susannah was bound to resent him if he dragged her across a continent, away from her family and friends. How would she feel about his most recent occupation?

"Would you not agree, Captain?" Lord Ponsby asked.

Winston blinked with a start. "I beg your pardon, I have let my thoughts wander. What was the question?"

"Are you all right?" Susannah asked. "You look a bit peeked."

"Just a bit chilled," Winston said. He did not like the way Susannah's gaze narrowed upon him, as if she could detect his thoughts simply by staring at him.

"Captain, you mustn't catch a chill. I shall have Cook make up a draught for you to take. She is very talented with medicinal herbs. The housekeeper can fetch it for you after our tea."

Winston realized that a chance to wander about Dunsford House unencumbered had presented itself. "Miss Dunsford, please do not trouble your housekeeper. Since I am rather fascinated by what goes into these draughts, would you mind terribly if I ventured down to the kitchens to request it myself?"

"Oh, but I would never impose on you," Miss Dunsford said, clearly thinking him odd for requesting such a thing.

He looked at Ponsby for help. The young lord understood. "Do let him go. I vow I do not wish to hear again how he managed to skip his stone over seven times."

Miss Dunsford giggled. Susannah gave him a questioning look, which he ignored.

Once out of the drawing room, Winston darted down the empty hallway to the next door. Silently he opened it and looked inside. An unoccupied library.

Slipping quietly into the room, he methodically ran his hands along the wall, the bookshelves, and behind paintings in an attempt to find a hidden compartment. Nothing.

Next he searched the drawers of small tables, under cushions of chairs and sofas and even under the Aubusson carpet. Still nothing. Standing up, he scanned the ceiling and the walls more closely. There was nothing to find, so he mentally checked off the room. He looked at his pocket watch. He'd been gone ten minutes.

After exiting, he rushed along the hall. Blast, he'd need more time to look for that letter than stolen excuses to leave Miss Dunsford's company. He would have to make do with the time that he had. He kept his eyes trained upon the hallway walls, stopping to check behind paintings. Nothing but solid wall presented itself. He stopped a chambermaid on her way up the stairs for directions to the kitchens. He had to fetch his draught and be back in the drawing room before long.

Susannah sat with a cup of steaming tea, wondering what was taking Winston so long. It had been almost half of an hour since he had left. She glanced at Miss Dunsford, who seemed almost relieved at Winston's absence. Lord Ponsby appeared pulled by which lady to bestow his attention upon. He seemed much more comfortable talking to Miss Dunsford.

In Susannah's opinion, the two of them made a near perfect match. They had much more in common with each other, and they spoke easily enough. Susannah's attention was diverted when Winston finally walked into the drawing room with a small bottle in his hand.

"I beg your pardon for arriving after the tea cart,"

Winston said. "I took a wrong turn on my way to the kitchens, but your cook did in fact have just the thing for my chills."

"Do not worry, Captain. The tea is still hot, so you have not missed a thing." Miss Dunsford started to get up from her chair.

"Oh, do stay, Miss Dunsford, and finish your comfortable coze with Lord Ponsby," Susannah said quickly. "I am closer to the cart and perfectly happy to pour Captain Jeffries his tea."

Miss Dunsford looked surprised, but she agreed. "Very well, please do."

Susannah turned to Winston. "Let me see if I remember how you take it. A lump of sugar and generous with the milk, is that so?"

"It is," he said quietly.

Susannah went about the business of pouring tea under Winston's watchful gaze. She took her time stirring the hot bohea in order to prolong the process and keep Winston's attention. Finally she held out the finished product to him. "There, just the way you like it."

He reached for the cup, and their fingers touched. "Thank you."

Susannah stared into his eyes. In a blink of the eye, she felt like the years had melted away, and they stood as they had once done at Sheldrake Hall. Only now there was something different in the depths of Winston's gaze—something dark and painful. Her heart ached for him when she noticed the bluish tint just below his eyes. Something was not quite right with him, and she wondered what the war had done to him.

"I say, I take my tea exactly opposite." Lord Ponsby's voice intruded. "Plenty of sugar and just a drop of milk."

"Never could abide anything too sweet," Winston said as he took a seat as far away from Susannah as possible. He sat near Miss Dunsford.

The moment was gone, but the connection she felt with him stayed strong. They were meant for one another, but something held Winston back from believing it. She wondered what it could be and how she would conquer it.

"Did you hear about Lord Elgin's Marbles?" Miss Dunsford asked Susannah, but her eyes strayed to Lord Ponsby.

"Are those the statues taken from the Parthenon?" Susannah asked distractedly, her thoughts still focused on Winston.

"Yes. The latest *on dit* is that Lord Elgin plans to sell the artifacts to England." Miss Dunsford leaned forward and whispered, "I think he needs the ready."

Susannah nodded even though she had never met Lord Elgin and knew even less about him. She did remember Sheldrake telling Olivia about the Elgin Marble debate going on in Parliament. Eager to share her knowledge of events in front of Winston, she added, "Perhaps we should endeavor to see them before they are turned over to Parliament. My brother-in-law said there are those in the House of Commons who think they should be returned to Greece."

"They do belong back in Greece," Winston said with conviction.

"Have you seen them?" Susannah asked.

"No."

"I have," Lord Ponsby said. "Seems like a lot of excitement over a bit of marble."

"Marble? They have religious as well as historic significance." Winston set down his cup of tea upon the small table next to his chair. "And just because some lord of the realm had the blunt to buy them, doesn't make it right for him to take them. I heard that he had to break some of them just to load them."

"Strong sentiments," Lord Ponsby said. "I visited the Parthenon on my Grand Tour," Lord Ponsby explained. "It appeared no worse for wear without Elgin's Marbles."

Susannah sat quietly as the two men debated the subject. Throughout the exchange, Susannah noticed that Miss Dunsford listened eagerly. She added intelligent comments where she could. Perhaps she had judged the young lady too harshly because of Winston's interest in her.

"Lord Ponsby, you know Lord Elgin," Miss Dunsford said. "Perhaps you could arrange a private showing for all of us."

"Yes, do," Susannah added with real enthusiasm. "What a wonderful idea."

"What say you, Captain?" Lord Ponsby asked.

"I could not think of a more agreeable adventure for the four of us." He grinned directly at Miss Dunsford, who blushed prettily, even though she glanced quickly at Lord Ponsby.

"Nicely put, Captain Jeffries," Miss Dunsford finally said.

Susannah sipped her tea, her mind working furiously. Perhaps she should befriend Miss Dunsford. First, she would have to delicately inform her rival that she had no designs upon Lord Ponsby. Susannah thought Miss Dunsford nursed a serious *tendre* for Lord Ponsby. Before she dare take the diminutive Miss Dunsford into her confidence, she would make certain which gentleman Miss Dunsford desired.

Finally they took their leave, and the short carriage

ride home was practically a silent one. Susannah glanced back at Winston in the rear seat. He looked tired. In fact his eyelids closed low several times. Once in front of Sheldrake's town house, Susannah allowed Lord Ponsby to help her down.

She turned to Winston, who nearly slumped on the seat. Poor dear, she thought as she gazed at his sleeping form. "Should we not wake him?" she asked Lord Ponsby.

"No. He looks comfortable, and if the truth be told, I do not think the man gets enough sleep."

Susannah fretted over Lord Ponsby's statement. The dark smudges under Winston's eyes were not her imagination. She was determined to find out what had happened to change the carefree officer with a twinkle of merriment in his eyes that was the Captain Jeffries she had met at Sheldrake Hall.

Winston shook inside. Blood ran down his left hand, and it hurt terribly. He wrapped his cravat around it to stop the flow, but in no time the white linen was soaked to a crimson red. He had to hurry. He searched the man's body, but could not find the documents from Napoleon. They were the reason he had killed the man. They had to be there!

"No!" Winston came awake with a jerk that almost took him out of the carriage seat and onto the floor. He steadied himself, but his head pounded. He was not sure where he was. Sweat ran down his back and trickled across his forehead. He'd been dreaming.

Susannah!

He stood up and looked around in sheer panic. No one was in sight, thank God. Relief flooded his being, making him weak, in the knees. The carriage was parked outside of Susannah's town house. She had not seen him. She did not know.

He leaned back against the seat and mopped his brow with his hand. The nightmares were getting worse, and they were more vivid. It was as if he was there, feeling it all over again. He rubbed his left hand. By Jove, it throbbed!

He looked up as he heard the click of the door. Ponsby skipped down the steps, and then stopped short when he saw Winston.

"My word, what happened to you?"

"I fell asleep," Winston said with caution.

"But you're sweating like you'd been sparring at Gentleman Jackson's."

"The sunshine." Winston tried to cover his shakiness with bravado. "I got deuced hot, lying here."

Lord Ponsby looked at him as if he was sick. "You had better take that draught the Dunsfords' cook gave you. It is not hot outside today, and you took a chill inside. I think you may be coming down with a fever. In fact, I shall take you home this minute. You should go straight to bed."

Winston nearly chuckled at the worried look upon Ponsby's face. "Perhaps you are correct," he said. "With a little rest, I should be right as rain." Winston truly wanted a good night's rest, but he was afraid to sleep.

Wednesday evening came with the opening night of Almack's assembly rooms. Winston surveyed the large ballroom. Almack's was nearly filled to capacity with young ladies dressed in white and gentlemen dressed in black coats and ivory knee breeches. Ponsby made sure they had arrived fashionably late. Winston had been chomping at the bit to leave White's, where they had played a few rounds of casino. He had some serious courting to do with Miss Dunsford. "I think we are perhaps too late," Winston said.

"Never appear overly eager, Captain."

"I fear I have yet to learn the rules of society courtship." Winston adjusted his coat and watched his step as he took the stairs. He was never one for wearing evening pumps, either.

"Cheer up." Ponsby patted him on the back. "My sister tells me you are making quite a stir among the young ladies. You are a common topic of discussion."

Winston nearly rolled his eyes. He realized the truth of Ponsby's statement when many a young misses' gaze turned upon him as he walked by. He nearly laughed aloud at the absurdity of it all. "Yes, well. The one I must court has no interest, so what does it matter for the rest."

"My goodness, Captain, have you no thoughts of marriage?"

"No, I'll not marry." Winston absently rubbed his scarred hand. How could he ever expect a woman to love him if she knew what he had done? "And what of you? Are you looking for a wife?"

"Actually, I am. It's time I set up my nursery and ensure the security of my family line. My father has not been well, and I shall more than likely inherit the earldom sooner than I had hoped. If something were to happen to me before I produced an heir, my cousin would inherit, much to my father's displeasure. There has never been a break from father to son."

"Duty," Winston murmured.

"Aye," Ponsby sighed.

"Lord Ponsby and Captain Jeffries. Good Evening." Susannah appeared from behind them.

"Miss Lacey, how ravishing you look." Ponsby bent over her exquisitely gloved hand.

Winston mentally agreed. She looked stunning. "Miss Lacey."

Susannah and Ponsby chatted briefly about the anticipated trip to view Elgin's Marbles. Winston wondered if Ponsby had settled on Susannah as his choice for a bride. Surprisingly, the thought did not sit well with him. Ponsby was an honorable man who Winston had encouraged Susannah to pursue, but deep inside, the idea of Susannah with any man other than himself, was an unwelcome one. The feeling was so strong that Winston had to get away from her.

"Please excuse me," he said with a brief bow. He forced himself to ignore the look of disappointment on Susannah's face. He needed to search out Miss Dunsford. She was his mission, she was the ticket to his future post in India, and *she* was the lady he needed to concentrate on for pity's sake. It was high time he stopped allowing Susannah to distract him. He had a specific reason for being in London. Duty, he thought bitterly. He had his bloody duty to do.

Susannah tried to pay heed to Lord Ponsby, but it was proving difficult. Why had Winston walked away? Out of the corner of her eye, she watched him approach Miss Dunsford, where he scribbled on her dance card.

She prayed silently that he had not scratched his name next to Miss Dunsford's supper dance. Susannah had purposefully left that dance open on her card in hopes of taking supper with Winston. The waltz was out, since this was her first ball. She had not yet gained permission from the Lady Patronesses of Almack's. Lord Ponsby had graciously signed his name to sit out with her. An idea took shape in her mind.

"Come, Lord Ponsby," she said as she took his arm to lead him. "Let us pay our respects to Miss Dunsford."

"Good evening, Miss Dunsford. Captain." Susannah had nearly run into them.

"Miss Lacey, Lord Ponsby." Miss Dunsford's voice softened considerably when she looked upon Lord Ponsby.

"I say, what dances have you scheduled with Captain Jeffries?" Susannah did not bother with subtlety.

Miss Dunsford narrowed her gaze. "The waltz and the supper dance."

Susannah was not the least bit happy about the waltz, but the supper dance could yet be saved. "How convenient, as Lord Ponsby has promised me the supper dance as well." Susannah had not reserved that dance but knew Lord Ponsby would not refuse. "Would you join us?"

Again, that narrowed gaze, as if Miss Dunsford were trying to figure out what she was about. Susannah smiled sweetly and gazed purposefully into her eyes in order to send a mental message.

It worked since Miss Dunsford smiled brilliantly in return. "I should like that above all things."

"Very well, then. Once again, we are a foursome," Lord Ponsby said.

Susannah looked triumphantly at Winston.

"You don't quit, do you," he whispered for her ears alone.

"I will not, not until I have won."

One of her partners for a cotillion stood at her elbow. "Miss Lacey, our dance I believe."

"Of course." She let the young gentleman lead her into the set. She was completely flustered by Winston.

It was not his words, but the look in his eyes that had her heart racing. Hope soared within her breast.

Winston watched as Susannah joined the formation of the dance. She wore a smile of genuine enjoyment as she glided in and out of the dance. She was neither coy nor flirtatious. Susannah Lacey was direct in her speech and manner. In fact, she was sheer perfection. It was no wonder that her dance card was full, save for the supper dance, and that he knew she had saved for him. But even though he had asked Miss Dunsford, Susannah had gotten her way by making it a foursome.

Might he be wrong in his decision to stay away from her? He knew that she would bring nothing but joy to his life. The temptation to pursue Susannah was a tangible thing that made his skin itch with the wanting of it. Perhaps it was the farce of parading about like a war hero, rich and ready to settle down, that made him wish with all his being that it was true. Reality forced its way into his thoughts. He was dreaming if he thought he could make Susannah happy. Looking around at the shimmering grandeur of society, he knew the truth—he had little to offer her.

The evening progressed, and Winston did his duty to dance with as many eligible young ladies as possible. He was careful to dance only twice with Miss Dunsford. He hoped that he sent a clear message by singling her out. His intent was serious pursuit. The fact that when he had waltzed with Miss Dunsford, she seemed to be miles away and completely uninterested in him was an obstacle he knew he would have to work harder at overcoming. His mission was at stake. He had to search her father's estate thoroughly, and only a welcomed suitor could call on her.

*　　*　　*

Miss Caroline Dunsford put on her pelisse. The opening evening at Almack's had ended in an interesting turn of events, she thought. She had danced the supper dance with Captain Jeffries and yet Miss Lacey had coaxed Lord Ponsby into making their supper a foursome.

She wondered what Miss Lacey was about. By all appearances, Captain Jeffries was the man Miss Lacey favored, and yet she could not be certain of how deeply the young lady's affections were engaged. She could simply be flirting with Captain Jeffries, as many a young miss was wont to do with a military man. Caroline soon realized that Lord Ponsby did not look terribly concerned by Miss Lacey's interest in the captain, and Caroline's heart had swelled with hope. In fact, Lord Ponsby had spent most of the supper talking to her instead of Miss Lacey.

They had had a wonderful conversation about Italy. Lord Ponsby had traveled extensively when he made his Grand Tour. She was thrilled to find that they had much in common. Lord Ponsby was the perfect gentleman, one who planned to stay in town instead of rusticating in the country over half of the year. He would no doubt need an experienced hostess to entertain for his guests, especially once he inherited his title.

Caroline smiled. She had extensive experience in that quarter. She effectively ran Dunsford House and acted as hostess for her father's many gatherings of political and diplomatic acquaintances, as well as close friends. She would make the perfect wife for Lord Ponsby. She only needed to make him see the obvious, as well.

Chapter Six

*T*he following day proved to be mild but overcast. Susannah was grateful that it was not raining. She walked beside Olivia along the crowded Bond Street shops, practically humming.

"I take it from your sunny disposition this morning that your pursuit of Captain Jeffries is going well," Olivia said quietly as the two of them searched through a bin of gloves.

"I believe I am making progress," Susannah said. Even Miss Dunsford appeared pleased with the way things had turned out last night. The four of them had quite enjoyed themselves.

"I see." Olivia reached deep inside the bin to pull out a buff-colored pair of fine leather gloves. "But I heard that he has singled out the Dunsford girl."

"He has, and I cannot figure out why exactly. I think Miss Dunsford is hopelessly in love with Lord Ponsby." Susannah picked up a charming Huntley bonnet of plaid that was trimmed with a rosette and three feathers. "Oh, do look at this. Is it not the very thing?"

"It becomes you," Olivia said as she gathered several pairs of gloves. "Do you think he has feelings for Miss Dunsford?"

"No," she answered her sister. "I do not think he cares a whit for her. He does the poorest job of flirtation I have ever witnessed. He is stiffer than a board, and his eyes betray him, to me at least. I catch him often looking at me, and there is longing there. At first I used to think I was imagining it, that I wished for it to be there. But now I know it is real. I will capture Winston's heart yet."

Olivia reached out and gave her hand a squeeze. "Good for you, dear. But what of Lord Ponsby?"

"He is a nice gentleman to be sure, but I do not think he quite knows what he wants. I cannot think his feelings are in the least engaged toward me."

"I am sure you are correct."

Susannah looked around in order to find a matching scarf of plaid, when she noticed the door to the shop had opened and Miss Dunsford appeared. "Miss Dunsford, good morning," she called.

Miss Dunsford's smile was genuine as she walked up to them. "Good morning. How are you this morning?"

"Wonderful," Susannah said. The three spoke briefly until Susannah pulled Miss Dunsford aside. "I know this is hardly the place, but may I ask you something of a personal nature?"

Miss Dunsford looked surprised but agreed, "Of course."

"Very well." Susannah glanced at her sister, who stood talking with a shopkeeper about a bolt of light green silk. "I cannot tell you how delighted I am to have a chance to ask you about last night's supper. I had planned to be delicate, but I simply must say it straight out. Do you favor Captain Jeffries or Lord Ponsby?"

"Why Lord Ponsby, of course." Miss Dunsford suddenly looked unsure, almost stricken. "Do not say that you do as well."

Susannah reached out and grabbed hold of Miss Dunsford's gloved hand. "Oh, I could hug you right here. I am completely lost to Captain Jeffries. No other man will do."

Miss Dunsford patted her hand in agreement. "I do know exactly how you feel. Once I met Lord Ponsby, I found all other gentlemen lacking by comparison. But he does not quite know that I exist." She dropped her gaze.

"Nonsense," Susannah gave her hand a squeeze of encouragement. "I do not believe he knows quite what he is about as of yet. I have a proposition for you. I do hope you will not think me bold, but if we joined forces, perhaps we could help each other."

Miss Dunsford grinned, which produced dimples in each cheek. "A wise plan of action," she said. "You must come to my house for luncheon so that we may discuss the matter further, and you must call me Caroline."

"I shall be there, if you call me Susannah. What time?"

Miss Dunsford checked the watch pinned to her bodice. "Shall we say two?"

"Until two," she said with a smile.

Susannah remained seated in Caroline Dunsford's large drawing room as various gentlemen made their calls. She meant to leave, but Caroline had asked that she stay. Susannah was amazed to discover that Caroline was a lonely young lady. She had no siblings, her mother had died three years ago, and her father often kept to himself due to his busy schedule with Parliament or other business matters. The aloofness that Caroline portrayed to the *ton* was actually a cover for her shyness. Caroline Dunsford was not nearly as happy as a peer of the realm's daughter should be.

They had spent an enjoyable luncheon. Afterward, Susannah had been given a complete tour of Dunsford House. The home was huge, with two libraries, an enormous office, and a full-sized ballroom off of the main dining room.

Susannah looked about the room that was filled with callers and Caroline's abigail who acted as chaperon. Some of the gentlemen were surprised to see Susannah, stating that they had left cards at Sheldrake's town house moments beforehand. It was not long before Winston arrived.

He also looked surprised to see her and nodded his greeting before he gave a handful of posies meant for Caroline to her abigail.

"Good afternoon, Winston," Susannah whispered when he stood within earshot of her.

"Miss Lacey," he said. "What brings you here?"

"Making plans with Miss Dunsford." She smiled when he looked at her with a mixture of amusement and confusion.

"I did not realize that you two were friends," he said. "If you will excuse me, I must pay my respects to her."

"Of course." She watched closely as Winston made his rounds. Caroline paid him no more attention than the other gentlemen seated around her. Susannah soon found herself with a small circle of her own callers. Sometime later, Lord Ponsby arrived and took a seat near her.

"Good afternoon, Miss Lacey," Lord Ponsby said. "I stopped to see you, and your aunt said that I would

find you here. I did not realize that you and Miss
Dunsford had become friends."

"We have and she is a delightful young lady, do
you not agree?" Susannah leaned toward him as she
asked.

Lord Ponsby answered quickly. "Yes, quite so, indeed she is."

"And yet you met her last year," Susannah pried.
She wanted to find out what Lord Ponsby thought of
Caroline and promote her new friend where she could.

"Yes, at the opening ball at Almack's. She was quite
the dignified young lady." Lord Ponsby rubbed his
chin.

"She has had many admirers call upon her today."
Susannah watched Lord Ponsby closely in order to
gauge his reaction, but there was none. Oh, dear, she
thought. Lord Ponsby did not appear moved by this
news at all. Perhaps all Lord Ponsby needed was more
time in Caroline's company without any distractions.

The callers had thinned considerably. Most had
taken their leave. Even Winston was gone, and her
heart sank. He had not said good-bye. An ache of
disappointment tore at her heart. There was nothing
to be done but concentrate on helping Caroline. If she
could contrive to exit the room and leave Caroline
alone with Lord Ponsby, it might move matters along
between them.

She wondered what excuse she could give, when a
thought struck her. Carefully, she placed the leg of
the chair she sat upon over the hem of her gown,
and shifted in her seat, tearing her dress. "Oh," she
exclaimed. "Do forgive me, but I have just caught my
hem. Miss Dunsford, do be a dear and tell me where
I may go to repair it."

"The third door to the left, down the hallway. My

needlework basket is on the divan where I left it this morning. There is every color of thread there."

"Thank you." Susannah rose awkwardly. She gave a slight curtsy to Lord Ponsby, whose disapproving expression gave her pause. Had she been caught? Or did he think her unrefined for remarking on the tear? She did not care to contemplate. Caroline needed her help. She excused herself, leaving the two alone save for the chaperon.

Caroline fluffed her gown. Lord Ponsby looked like a fish out of water, the poor man. An awkward silence settled upon them, which was uncommon, since they usually carried on quite comfortably. Her abigail sat knitting in the corner. Lord Ponsby was aware of their chaperon and that appeared to add to his discomfort. What on earth could she do to start a conversation? She looked upon the far table. "Lord Ponsby, do you play cribbage?"

"Uh, why, yes, I do."

"Would you like to play?" she asked.

"Certainly." He came near and offered her his arm.

She glanced up into his eyes and nearly stopped breathing. The room and the furnishings about them faded away. Caroline saw only Lord Ponsby. The expression on his face made her heart race. She thought that he looked at her as if seeing her for the first time. She realized that they stood in the middle of the drawing room, gazing at one another.

Her abigail coughed genteelly.

"Cribbage," Caroline said. "Come, let us play until Miss Lacey returns."

Susannah walked down the hallway, counting the doors until she reached her destination. She entered the cozy morning room and spotted the opened basket of thread on the couch, as Caroline had said. She sat down with a bounce, lifting the hem of her skirt into her lap. She nearly pricked her finger threading the needle when the door opened and Winston entered quietly.

"I thought you had left," Susannah said.

He nearly jumped. "Susannah," he said with a whisper. His deep brown eyes gleamed as his gaze swept her exposed ankle.

"I tore my hem," she said, pleased with the fact that Winston was staring.

"I seem to have gotten turned around on my way out," he said, his voice thick.

Confused, she said, "You have been gone awhile."

He hesitated. "I've been lost."

Susannah narrowed her gaze. It did not make sense. "Could you not have asked a servant?"

"Didn't see any. Then I saw you walk this way, and I wondered what you were up to." He stood with both hands firmly clasped behind his back.

"Me?" She hadn't stopped sewing, but her heart raced at his admission that he had sought her out. She forgot all about him being lost. "Now you know. I am merely repairing my gown."

Winston remained standing silently watching her.

"You may sit down," she offered quietly.

"I should leave. It would not do if anyone found us like this."

"As if anyone would. It shall only take me a moment to finish this hem, and we can return to the drawing room. Lord Ponsby is visiting."

"Is he?" He sounded surprised, but still he remained standing.

Susannah blathered on. "The flowers you brought

Miss Dunsford are very pretty," she said as she made neat little stitches.

"I bought them from a street vendor." He shifted as if itching to be gone. "I must own that I was surprised to see you here."

"Why?" Her hem was nearly finished.

"I did not realize you and Miss Dunsford were friends."

"We became fast friends today."

An awkward silence settled over them. Susannah desperately wanted to keep Winston in this room but knew she could not if she was to keep her reputation in tact. Besides, he appeared hesitant to leave.

Susannah tied off the last knot and bit the thread all under Winston's gaze. It was unnerving and exhilarating at the same moment. Susannah stood and shook out her skirts. "There, that should do until I am home." She walked toward Winston but she did not pay attention to where she stepped. She stubbed her toe on the leg of a heavy chaise lounge in her path. "Ouch!" she cried out.

"What is it?" His arms were about her, helping her to sit down on the chaise.

Tears welled up in her eyes, and she grit her teeth. "I stubbed my toe, and it hurts like the very devil!" She tried to grab hold of her toe.

"Here," he said. "Let me." He bent and picked up her right foot. "Is it this one?"

"Yes," she groaned, wiping away a tear.

He unlaced her slipper in a very soldierly fashion, quick and precise. Then he felt along her foot down to her toes. "Wiggle them if you can," he said.

She did as she was bid, and nearly giggled even though it still hurt. She found it difficult to breath as he touched her.

"Is it this one?" He bent her littlest toe.

This time she did giggle. It tickled. "Yes." She laughed again.

He looked up, a smile in his eyes. "I do not think it is broken. You must take care, Susannah, or you'll be tripping at some grand event."

"But I am very careful to walk slowly in public. I make certain that I have a wide berth before I even move."

He laughed, and the sound of it filled the room and her heart. Her foot still rested in his palm, her slipper forgotten. His smile died as he looked at her, his gaze intense. She reached for his hand. "I have missed you so," Susannah said in a quiet voice.

Winston wanted to run away from her, but he couldn't. He knelt with her foot upon his knee and her hands entwined in his own, and by Jove, he wanted to kiss her. He had missed her, too. The memories of their first meeting had tugged at his heart with bittersweet longing. The letters they had once exchanged promised more than mere friendship, he knew. They were sweet as honey. And now here they were, and still her sweetness beckoned to him like a bee come home to the hive.

"You are so beautiful," he thought, and then realized he had said it aloud to her.

She closed her eyes and leaned toward him. He concentrated on those lips he so frantically wanted to feel under his own. Just one taste of her was all he needed, and then perhaps he could finally leave her alone. He reached up to caress her soft cheek with his left hand and froze.

He stared at his hand. His filthy scarred hand touched the pure and innocent cheek of Susannah's face, and he nearly groaned with shame. He felt as if time had stopped, and he was disconnected from himself. In the blink of his eye, he envisioned himself telling her just how he had earned that scar. In his mind, he could see her trusting eyes turn fearful of him as she recoiled from him in disgust.

"Winston, what is it?" Susannah's voice intruded on his vision.

He realized what a fool he was to think he could handle being anywhere near Susannah Lacey. "Nothing." He leaned back on his haunches and looked about for her slipper.

"Please, tell me what is wrong? What were you thinking just then?"

"Susannah, we must go back." He quickly put her slipper on her foot and tied the laces into a tight bow. Then he stood and held out his hand to her.

She took it, but confusion and disappointment were written upon her face. In her eyes, he read the hurt. It was just as well that he had caught himself in time. He liked to think he was being noble by protecting Susannah from himself. If the truth were told, he protected himself from her and the ravishing grown woman she'd become.

They walked silently down the hallway, and Winston cursed his weakness. If he did not focus on his mission and the task at hand, he'd lose his post to India. They stopped just outside of the drawing room, and Winston took a deep breath. He glanced at Susannah, which was a mistake. She was bravely trying to smile, but she looked crushed. Winston felt like dirt to have done that to her. He gave her an encouraging nod and entered the room.

"Ah, Captain Jeffries." Miss Dunsford stood. "I thought you had left."

"I, uh, forgot my gloves," Winston lied. "Good day, Ponsby."

"Captain." Lord Ponsby nodded.

Susannah tried to regain her composure. Her insides felt as if someone had stirred them, and her head ached as she attempted to rein in her emotions.

"I was just telling Miss Dunsford that I have arranged for a private showing of the Marbles at Lord Elgin's house, on Park Lane. He warned me not to wear our best clothing, since the shed where he has the antiquities housed is damp and dusty."

"How wonderful." Susannah tried to sound enthusiastic, but knew she failed. Nothing made sense. Winston cared for her, yet he would not give in and act upon his feelings. "When is the showing?" she asked.

"A week from today. If we arrive late morning, Elgin will provide us with a light repast served out of doors, weather permiting, for luncheon."

"Well-done, Ponsby," Winston added. He had taken a seat near Caroline, putting as much distance between them as possible. He would not look at her.

Susannah let out a sigh. Capturing Winston's love was not going to be easy.

Susannah sat by the window of her chamber that overlooked the street and wiped her eyes with a cool cloth. People and carriages meandered about, but she did not see them. She stared out of the window wallowing in self-pity. She had been crying and she could not allow anyone to know, especially Sheldrake.

Almost an entire week had passed and not once had she talked privately with Winston. At parties, dinners, and balls, he said nothing more than a polite good evening. He had not called upon her with Lord

Ponsby, and when she visited Caroline's house if Winston arrived, he kept his distance from her.

Winston had often been seen in the company of Caroline Dunsford, and rumors abounded that he planned to offer for her. Such *on dits* tore her heart in two. Olivia had hugged her often, and Sheldrake watched her closely. She had put on a cheerful front for the sake of everyone, and the strain was beginning to take its toll. If Winston offered for Caroline, she vowed she would never come out of this room.

A knock at the door brought her head up. "Come in," Susannah said with a thin voice.

"Miss Caroline Dunsford is here for you," a maid announced.

Susannah thought quickly, they could be more private in her chamber. "Please send her up."

In no time Caroline appeared in her doorway. "Oh, dear, Susannah, what have you done?" She rushed to her side.

"Whatever can you mean?" Susannah sniffed.

"You have been crying haven't you?" Caroline said.

"Is it that obvious?"

"And over Captain Jeffries, no doubt." Caroline removed her bonnet and placed it upon the writing desk. "What did you do to him? He has been courting me feverishly, and I cannot be rid of him!"

"He is not a bad man," Susannah defended him.

"Of course not, but even I can plainly see that it is *you* he desires. My goodness, he is afraid to look at you. And Lord Ponsby no longer accompanies Captain Jeffries when he calls upon me, so I have no defense against his advances."

"Has he tried to kiss you?" Susannah shuttered at the thought.

"He has not. He is a forgetful fellow. He is constantly leaving things behind. I think he has gone only to find him in the hallway looking for his hat or gloves or some such. Or he visits with Cook and has trouble finding his way back."

"Really?" Susannah thought that information very odd indeed, considering he claimed to be lost the day she repaired her hem. Something was not quite right.

Caroline sat down upon the bed with a sigh. "What are we going to do? The wrong gentlemen are courting us."

Susannah sat upon the bed next to her friend. She put her arm around Caroline's shoulders and gave her an encouraging squeeze. "I do not know. But we have to do something, tomorrow at Burlington House may be our only chance."

"You are right of course," Caroline agreed. "But what can we do? Do you think Lord Ponsby cares for you? I truly like you the best of all young ladies, Susannah, but if he loved you, I fear I could not bear it."

"Caroline, do not fret. Lord Ponsby has called upon me only as other gentlemen have. He has no warm feelings for me. In fact, I think he does not quite know what to do with me. He's more impressed by Sheldrake, I think."

"As Captain Jeffries seems obsessed with my father," Caroline said. "We are forever talking about him. But, I have told my father that Captain Jeffries is not for me."

"Then we must show these gentlemen the error of their ways. And it must be done tomorrow."

"How?" Caroline asked.

"How indeed." Susannah got up and paced the

floor, tapping her finger upon her lips. "We must endeavor to get them alone." She paused in her pacing. "I have it!"

"Do tell," Caroline said.

"Do you know if Burlington House has gardens?"

"Susannah, Lord Elgin has quite the maze of hedges. I have heard stories of picnics where the guests were lost for hours!" Caroline slid off the bed.

"Then that should be our plan. Perhaps after luncheon, we could suggest a walk in the maze, and then we must *get lost* within its walls each with our own gentleman."

"A perfect plan!" Caroline agreed.

"Let us hope it works," Susannah said.

Winston sat at his desk signing the papers for his partnership agreement as Ponsby lounged in a chair near the fireplace with a glass of fine French brandy in his hand.

"Where did you get this brandy? It is excellent." Ponsby swirled the amber liquid about.

"Fighting in France did have some advantages." Winston shuffled the papers.

Ponsby held his glass up in mock salute. "The French know how to make fine spirits."

"They do that," Winston answered distractedly as he scratched his name in the marked places.

"How did you manage to work for Lord Castlereagh, if I may ask?" Ponsby sat up straight in the chair and leaned forward in anticipation of a story.

Winston set his pen down. "It was after I was wounded at Toulouse." He leaned back. "I had lost a lot of blood and a fever set in. I was sent to Brussels to recover. There was no chance I'd return to the fighting any time soon. It looked as though the war was over, considering Napoleon had been sent to Elba. Lord Castlereagh approached me while he was in Brussels. He needed aid in gaining information. He did not believe Napoleon would take defeat. And blast, but he'd been correct.

"My services where engaged when he bought out my commission. I have been in the service of the Foreign Office for two years. I am promised a post to India when I complete this assignment," Winston explained. "I hope to once again be a real military captain."

"You have had quite an opportunity to serve England. You should be proud."

"I have paid a personal price that I fear England can never repay. Many times, I wish I had simply returned to my regiment," Winston muttered.

"But surely you have been well compensated for your efforts, much more so than mere Captain's pay," Lord Ponsby defended.

"I have, although my expenses have greatly increased as well. Even so, I look forward to a normal life. Some things are not worth the gold paid for them."

Winston knew he had to leave the subject alone due to the secrecy required of him. Ponsby had the notion shared by many Englishmen who had not gone to war. It was all honor, and heroics. Winston had heartily agreed until two years ago.

After taking the life of an innocent man in the name of duty, he found his actions a bitter draught to swallow. The memories haunted him.

At Lord Ponsby's silence, Winston finished signing the last paper. "Shall we take your barouche to view Elgin's Marbles?"

"Indeed we shall."

Winston hesitated before he said, "I thank you for staying clear of Miss Dunsford these last few days. I have focused on her alone, and I believe it will pay off."

"Have you found what you must be searching for?" Ponsby did not look up. He concentrated on swirling his drink.

Winston tread lightly. He could not burden Ponsby with the knowledge of what he was after, it would only complicate matters between them. "Not yet, but I am making progress. It is simply a matter of time before I find it."

"What will happen to her once your mission is complete?" Ponsby asked.

"Nothing." Winston did not like to think about how Miss Dunsford's life could change once her father was labeled a traitor. He couldn't.

"I am not stupid." Ponsby rose from his chair, his glass in hand. "I know this has to do with her father's diplomatic connections, but whatever it is that you search for, I hope you never find it."

Winston looked away and he ran his finger along the side of his desk. He could not quite meet Ponsby's eyes. "These things are never easy," he said quietly. "In the name of duty to King and Country, it must be done. Perhaps now you understand why I wish to leave this all behind for India."

Lord Ponsby nodded solemnly.

"Come." Winston slapped Ponsby upon the back. "Let us go to Gentleman Jackson's and sweat off our melancholy, for tomorrow we must woo the ladies."

Lord Ponsby sat before the fire in his undress. He was exhausted but content. He had gone several rounds with Jeffries in the ring at Gentleman Jackson's. He was a good fighter, but Jeffries was better, which was not surprising considering the man's military background. There was an intensity in how Winston Jeffries carried himself that made Ponsby push himself that much harder. The small gash over his eyebrow gave credence to his exertion. He had never before been cut while in the ring.

He sipped his tea and considered his situation. He was quite attracted to Miss Caroline Dunsford much to his chagrin and better judgment. Her father was being investigated for treason. It simply would not do to pursue such a lady. He had his title and position to consider, his loyalty to his family.

But her eyes were incredibly large and dark, and he wondered why he had never noticed how fine they were before. Caroline Dunsford had always seemed so cold and distant.

During last year's Season, many gentlemen had dubbed her the Ice Princess. There was nothing but fire in her eyes that afternoon in her drawing room. When she gazed at him, he found himself quite warmed. Had her chaperon been absent, he wondered if he would have done something about the invitation he read in her eyes. He wanted to feel her in his arms and find out if she was as fragile as she looked. He doubted she would break easily.

He was glad that Winston had asked him to stay away from her. It had given him time to think. It was time that he set up his nursery, and he needed to choose a wife by the end of the Season. Miss Lacey would make an admirable wife. What she lacked in sophistication, she more than made up for in kindness. But he had held back at the last moment from speaking to Lord Sheldrake.

The memory of staring into a pair of large, dark,

and enticingly feminine eyes kept him from asking Lord Sheldrake's permission to pay his addresses to Miss Lacey. Caroline Dunsford was everything he wanted in a future countess, plus she made his pulse race when he was near her. That reaction should carry some weight in his decision. He wanted to enjoy the begetting of heirs. But, Caroline Dunsford posed the problem of bringing scandal to his name, and that would never do.

Chapter Seven

Susannah took Lord Ponsby's offered hand to step into his carriage. Winston was already inside, seated next to Caroline. Susannah suffered the familiar flutter in her stomach when she saw him. "Good morning," Susannah said cheerfully. This outing was more than viewing Lord Elgin's Marbles; it was a chance to be with Winston—alone.

"Miss Lacey. You look well today," he said with a polite nod.

No matter how indifferent or matter of fact Winston tried to sound, Susannah felt deep satisfaction in catching the admiration in his gaze. She had chosen her morning dress and bonnet with utmost care. Her gown was of the palest blue muslin, with a matching spencer of celestial blue that nearly matched her eyes. She was indeed glad that the rain from the day before had stopped by night fall, giving the ground a chance to dry. She wore her best kid leather half boots.

Caroline looked like a fairy, Susannah decided. She was dressed in soft petal pink with a plumed bonnet that was exquisitely frivolous. Susannah knew that Lord Ponsby would be hard pressed not to take notice of her. Their plan of action was simple. They would lure the gentlemen into the maze, separate, and if all went well—get lost for hours.

They pulled in front of Burlington House, the home of Lord Elgin. In no time they entered the great hall with tall windows giving way to a view of Park Lane and Hyde Park just beyond. They were met by Lord Elgin's butler, Sims. He informed them that their host had been called away to a meeting in Parliament, but the tour would proceed as scheduled.

Susannah tried not to gawk at the various sculptures lining the hallway. The furnishings were simple, elegant even, but the nude Greek statuettes appeared completely out of place against traditional English decor.

"A bit overdone, don't you think?" Winston whispered near her ear.

She could not help the shiver of pleasure that rippled along her spine. She managed to nod. At least he was not going to ignore her as he had done this past week.

"Would you care to follow me?" Sims asked.

"Of course. Do lead on," Lord Ponsby replied.

Winston offered his arm to Caroline, which left Susannah to take the arm of a surprisingly hesitant Ponsby. Winston was loath to admit that in the week he had stayed away from Susannah, his attraction to her had only increased. He found it difficult to keep his gaze from admiring her. She looked lovely, he had expected that, but there was an excited expectancy about her that made him almost nervous.

What if Susannah had finally decided to encourage Lord Ponsby? He could not help but feel dissatisfied. Surely Ponsby would have told him if Susannah had shown any signs of favoring his pursuit.

Winston had made little progress with Miss Dunsford. He had approached her father to ask permission to pay his addresses to his daughter, but Dunsford had refused him on the basis that they would not suit. There was no point in going any further in his farce of courtship, yet what other options did he have to gain access to Dunsford House?

He followed the butler across the expanse of lawn toward the outbuilding that housed the Marbles. They entered the small stable-like structure, and Winston smelled mildew even though the doors remained open. Oil lamps had been lit and placed upon pedestals to cast more light than the small windows allowed. It seemed wrong that such magnificent sculptures were stored in such humble surroundings.

"May I touch it?" Susannah asked the tall butler.

"Certainly," Sims said. "That frieze depicts the battle of the Greeks against the centaurs."

"Half men and half horse," Winston provided when Susannah looked confused. "From Greek mythology."

She still looked unsure. "I know so little of either Greek or Roman mythology. I did not study the classics, but I wish I had. These depictions are fascinating."

She bent closely to examine a particular sculpture with real interest, and Winston let his gaze linger on her form. She was perfection, more beautiful than any Greek ideal cast in marble. Ponsby and Miss Dunsford wandered down the line with Sims.

"What a fascinating culture. Were the Greeks warlike?" she asked him.

"Not at all." He stood next to her. "They valued excellence above all things, excellence of the mind, body, and art. Whatever mankind strived for, the Greeks found contentment as long as they reached beyond their limits."

Susannah turned to face him. "You admire them," she said.

"Of course I do. Their society encouraged man to be more and cheered him on when he did so."

"You do not think England does the same for her people?"

Winston shook his head. She knew him well, and yet she could not know how he had changed, how he had regressed instead of progressed. He had lost something of himself that England and his spying took from him. "We are not exactly a progressive society, not when there is such poverty."

"I suppose not," she said quietly after some thought. "But there have been many improvements. Only look at the air balloons and steam ships. Your Greeks did not have those, I would wager."

"No, they did not." He smiled at her stubborn loyalty.

"And the music, what music can they boast of, I ask you," she said. Her hands now rested on her hips. "Even though you have been to Spain and France and elsewhere in Europe with Wellington, do you still long to travel?" she suddenly asked.

Dearest Susannah, he thought. The only reason England was a better place in his way of thinking was because she made it that way. "And you still do not wish to leave her soil."

"I have never had reason to." She looked like she wanted to say something, but kept quiet as they viewed the remaining pieces of marble tablets that once hung above the columns inside the Parthenon.

He noticed that they were completely alone, and

that was not good. Sims had ushered Miss Dunsford and Ponsby into another room. He could hear their voices and Miss Dunsford's occasional peal of delicate laughter. "Come, the tour is leaving us behind."

After their viewing of the Marbles, they returned to the main house, where luncheon was served upon the terrace. The day remained warm even though clouds clustered along the horizon. Winston let himself relax, as if he had no mission and no past. He cared only for the present, and he wanted to enjoy it. It was a dangerous feeling, he knew, but for one day he did not wish to care. He wanted a taste of normal life.

Miss Dunsford became more animated in Susannah's presence. Both ladies teased Ponsby about the cut above his eye from their sparring and his appetite for poached pears. Ponsby ate the fruit with such a complete look of contentment that even Winston laughed until his eyes watered.

"Here, try one of these," Winston offered to Susannah.

She looked doubtful. "What is it?"

"I think it is a Greek pastry. It is delightful." Winston popped another one in his mouth.

Susannah shook her head. "I will not like it."

"Come, now, Miss Lacey," he teased. "How can you know unless you have tried?"

"I simply know what I like and that does not resemble anything that I know that I like."

He felt slightly disappointed at her refusal. He wanted to be the one to introduce something new to her. But then he watched her laugh, and he felt a heady rush of desire pump through his veins. This reaction to her was the reason he had stayed away, he reminded himself. He could barely handle her presence without coming close to losing sight of his future.

Sitting on Lord Elgin's terrace in the sunshine, he wished the moment might last forever.

Susannah sighed with bliss. Winston looked like his old self again. He had become the carefree officer she had known at Sheldrake Hall. His eyes twinkled despite the dark circles that were a permanent fixture of his face. He laughed and smiled and even winked at her. She caught Caroline's gaze and nodded. Now was the time to put into action their plan.

"Come." Caroline stood up. "We must have a go at the maze."

Susannah clapped her hands in agreement. "Yes, we simply must while we are here."

Lord Ponsby agreed, and even Winston stood without complaint. The four of them scurried off the terrace once Lord Ponsby informed Sims of their plans.

"Here," Susannah said when she stood at the entrance of the maze. "I think we must enter here." A wall of hedges stretched out before them. The maze encompassed the entire lawn. It looked vast as well as deep. Flowers of all varieties had been planted and tended along the front and sides.

The plan to separate was simple. She would detain Winston until Caroline and Lord Ponsby were out of sight. Caroline promised to take the first turn west with Lord Ponsby so that she and Winston could head east. If all went accordingly, they would not see each other for at least an hour or more.

After they entered the maze, Susannah bent down. "My slipper has come undone," she explained to Winston, who waited patiently for her. She took her time. "There," she said when she finally tied a bow. She stood slowly. Caroline and Lord Ponsby were out of sight.

"I certainly would not like to see you trip and fall."

Winston offered her his arm. "You might ruin that pretty dress."

"Do you like it?" she asked.

"Course I do. It is a nice color." Winston looked as if he regretted the words that he had just spoken. "How are things progressing with Ponsby?"

He had changed the subject, but Susannah was not discouraged. In fact, she smiled at him. Perhaps it would be better if she left that particular question unanswered. Let him think what he wished. He had pushed the young lord toward her, encouraged his suit, let him now wish that he hadn't, she thought. "Look, they have gotten ahead of us, and I am not sure which turn they took." They stood before an intersection in the maze. The tall leafy bushes had been trimmed to perfection, yet they were thick. There was no way to peek through the dense growth to see through to the other side.

"Perhaps we should take the right turn," Winston offered.

And that would be the way Caroline had taken Lord Ponsby, Susannah thought. "No, I believe Miss Dunsford would have suggested a turn to the left."

"Then, let us go to the left," Winston said with a wink.

They walked in silence for the first few yards. She no longer held onto Winston's arm, since he had both his hands clasped firmly behind his back. He whistled a soft tune under his breath. Susannah felt a thrill of excitement race down her spine at the thought of spending time with him alone. He had not even tried to flirt with Caroline, today. Susannah was not about to contemplate the matter when she had the chance to push herself forward.

"Tell me about the places you have been while serving under Wellington," she asked.

"What do you wish to know?"

"Tell me about the weather. What did you do when you were not fighting?" She looked to see how he would react, but he took the questions in stride.

"Spain is a beautiful country. It is warm with endless sun-filled days. I believe I prefer warmer climates."

"Considering the dreadfully cold and wet spring we have had this year, I cannot say that I blame you."

"You do not mind the rain do you?" he asked her.

"No, truly I do not. But do go on and tell me more."

"When we were not fighting, we were marching, moving into position, and planning our assault. We had the French on the run, pushing them back toward Paris. We did not let up."

"You were very brave," Susannah whispered.

"Not at all. I was always afraid, but I could not show that to my men. They needed me to stay strong. My bravado kept them encouraged." His eyes had taken on a far-off look, as if he were on the battlefield in his mind. He finally asked, "What else did you wish to know?"

She reached out to touch his left hand. "Does it pain you to speak of the war?"

"No. But it is difficult to convey what it was like, and so I try not to embellish upon it." They continued walking slowly, aimlessly wandering through the corridors of greenery.

"Why do you look as if you have not slept soundly? Is it the war that troubles you so?"

He looked startled at her direct question. She had not meant to ask, but now that she had, she was glad. She wanted to help if she could.

"I have a lot on my mind, so I am restless at night." They came to another turn in the maze. He took the path to the right.

Susannah regretted her words. The relaxed Winston disappeared to be replaced with the edgy man she had come to expect. She was sorry for shattering his ease with her questioning but now that she had started, she found that she could not stop. "Does courting Miss Dunsford trouble you? You do not appear to have a *tendre* for her, and it must be quite obvious that she favors Lord Ponsby."

He stopped walking and faced her. "It is complicated," he said quietly.

She looked up into his eyes, squinting despite the broad rim of her straw bonnet. "I am a good listener."

He reached out and caressed her cheek. "Yes, you are and you always have been."

"Then, why did you not write to me after you fell at Toulouse? Did you think I would not understand then?"

"Susannah," he said with a deep sigh. "There are things I have done. . . ." His voice dropped low. She was not sure she even heard him.

She felt as if her breathing had ceased. Everything turned quiet accept for the pounding of her heart in her ears. She looked at his lips, and he looked at hers. He wanted to kiss her. She could feel it. She leaned forward and let her eyes fall closed. She waited for what seemed like a lifetime for his kiss, but nothing happened. She opened her eyes.

"You deserve better. Someone like Ponsby who has more to offer you," he muttered.

Raw irritation and disappointment burned through her, fueling a sharp retort. "Do you think I do not know my own mind, sir?"

"You are young."

"Ooohhhh," she fumed. "I am older than most of the young ladies making their come-out. I am a solid year older than your Miss Dunsford! I think it is *you*, who does not know your mind! How clear can I possibly be? If I wanted someone better than you, do you not think I would seek that man out?" She stamped her foot and then walked on past him.

"Susannah," he said, following her, "I did not intend to make you angry. Come, let us not spoil the day by arguing."

She turned to him with her finger pointed directly at his chest. "You have feelings for me, Winston Jeffries. Do not deny it! I am not interested in your noble sacrifice for my good. I am mistress of my own good, I thank you."

"Yes, but . . ."

She cut him off, her finger now poking into his chest for emphasis. "You want me, so why do you not just take me!" She realized how inappropriate her comment was when she saw his eyes darken. It was not quite what she had meant, but even so, she wanted to understand his hesitancy to be near her, to pursue her, to love her.

He looked at her with fury and desire, as if a private war waged inside of him. She worried that she had gone too far when she saw the muscles alongside of his jaw flex and tighten. He took hold of her shoulders and brought her roughly against him. His lips crashed against hers. His bruising kiss was brief, leaving her shaken when he let her go.

"There," he said. "Is that what you wanted?"

She stepped back, her mind numb and her insides reeling. Her lips throbbed and she felt horrible. This was not what she wanted at all. She felt close to tears.

"Susannah," he finally said with a voice laced with regret. "It is not so simple. Sometimes we cannot take what we want. What you and I want may not be what is best."

Her insides shook with disappointment. She thought that if only he kissed her, he would love her. But that was not what happened. He had punished her with his kiss, and she felt completely rebuked. She never imagined the complexity she would find in him. What was it about her that was not good for him?

"Only you have the power to make it simple, Winston. I am not the one complicating matters." She turned away from him before she did something so foolish as to throw herself at his feet. She had made a tactical error, and her only course was to retreat, but she would not surrender.

"This way, I think," Caroline said as she pulled Lord Ponsby by the hand. The day was gloriously like it should be this time of year, and she felt as if she would burst out in song like the birds in the walls of bushes that surrounded them. Lord Ponsby showed marked interest in her today. In fact, she had caught him staring at her on two occasions. He had quickly looked away, but she knew he had been looking at her, and that gave her considerable hope.

They came to another turn. She still had a hold of Lord Ponsby's hand. He did not seem to mind.

"Which way?" Lord Ponsby asked.

Caroline looked about. There was no sign of Susannah or Captain Jeffries. She glanced at Lord Ponsby, who wore an amused smile. She stared at his lips wondering what it would feel like to kiss him. Slightly flustered, she quickly looked up to meet his gaze. His soft blue eyes had deepened in color and intensity. He knew exactly what she had been thinking.

"Let us take this turn," she said, pulling him along to the left.

Lord Ponsby let her lead him about, but if the truth were told, he did not care if they ever got out of the maze. He was completely enchanted by this slip of a female who looked curiously like some flower fairy all dressed in pink and plumes. He could not believe he had ever thought her aloof. She was entirely animated, and warmth emanated from her. Her cheeks were flushed, and her dark eyes danced with curiosity.

They came to a twisting tunnel. The bushes had been entwined with rose vines that grew overhead. It was an incredible sight, and the newly opened blossoms filled the air with their heady scent.

"Oh! Look at the roses. They are my favorite flower, and this shade is perfection." She had let go of his hand and stared in awe at the roses above their heads.

"Shall I pick one for you?"

"Please do."

He reached up and plucked a nearly opened bud and brought it to his nose to inhale its sweetness. Perhaps because of the relaxed setting of the day or because he forgot that her father might be a traitor, he tucked the flower behind her ear.

She looked up at him, her eyes huge and shining.

"The perfect shade is the blush of your cheek. Next to you, the rose does not compare." He could not believe such a statement had fallen from his lips, but it had. He found that he meant every word. Miss Caroline Dunsford was a lovely young woman. She was tiny and fragile-looking, with skin of cream, and her feminine allure was hitting him straight between the eyes.

She responded to his compliment in a manner he

would not have expected. Instead of fluttering her eyes or playing coy, she stepped closer to him. She placed both her hands upon his chest. "Thank you, Lord Ponsby. I have never been paid a prettier compliment."

"You are most welcome," he murmured. His gaze rested upon her full lips, but he caught himself in time. He could not risk a kiss. It would prove disastrous to compromise her in such a manner. He was not in a position to do the honorable thing by her, not yet at least. Not until her father's loyalties were proven as true to England.

Chapter Eight

*W*inston stepped out of the tub in his dressing room. He toweled his hair, rubbing furiously and cursing himself as an idiot. Susannah had effectively tipped his world upside down, and she did not fight fair. Neither did he, his conscience nagged. He had no right to treat her poorly regardless of his frustration. He had no idea what came over him to kiss her so harshly. He wanted Susannah, but knew better than to think there could be a happy future for them.

She had guarded the image of what he once had been in her sweet little heart. He could not change his past nor could he go back to being the idealistic soldier Susannah had fallen in love with. He padded across his dressing room as Pegston laid out his evening clothes.

"Did ye have a good nap?" Pegston asked.

"Fair enough." Winston stepped into the black breeches his valet held out for him.

After coming home from Lord Elgin's, Winston sat in his study with a glass of brandy and had fallen asleep. He had slept soundly, too, until his dreams were torn up with visions of Susannah Lacey searching among the dead and wounded soldiers. She had been dressed in gold, and the sun shone from the ends of her hair, the tops of her bare toes and fingertips. She smiled the entire time as she turned over bloodied and maimed bodies to see their faces. He had come awake with a start when his empty glass fell from the table to shatter on the floor.

"You look better, you do." Pegston helped him with a fine linen shirt.

He stood still as his valet tied a perfectly formed cravat in the style of the mathematical knot. After being trussed up into his evening coat of black velvet, Winston was ready for Almack's. He checked his watch before slipping it into his waistcoat pocket. He did not wish to be too late.

Walking the short distance from his town house to Almack's assembly rooms on Kings Street, he considered his options. His courtship of Miss Dunsford was doomed from the start. He was no further ahead in finding the letter. It was going to take far longer than he anticipated searching for it. He had to use Ponsby from now on to get him into Dunsford House. He'd think up something in order to roam the halls freely.

And then there was Susannah. He had no idea what he was going to do about her.

Susannah watched the doorway, but still Winston had not arrived. Caroline stood ringing her hands with impatience, which told her that Lord Ponsby had not arrived yet, either.

"I do hope Lord Ponsby shows," Caroline said softly.

"He will."

"He must," Caroline said.

Susannah noticed Winston as soon as he entered the ballroom. It was almost as if the very air changed when she saw him. Her breathing always became labored. He carried himself with authority as he walked across the room. He was devastatingly handsome even though his expression was serious. She wondered if he looked this way before he went into battle. She trembled at the memory of his kiss, feeling both nervous and excited. Her next move had to be right.

Winston approached them. "Good evening, ladies."

Susannah curtsied, but her voice had escaped her.

"Miss Lacey, perhaps you might grant me the honor of saving a waltz?" he asked.

Susannah's mouth dropped slightly open. "Yes, of course." She glanced at Caroline, who gave her an encouraging smile.

"You have been granted permission, have you not?" he asked.

The scent of his cologne beckoned her to step closer to him. She swallowed hard. "I have this very evening."

"Good. We will have a chance to talk." He bowed before turning his attention toward Caroline.

Susannah's breathing returned to normal, and her soaring hope fell back to earth. He wanted to talk, and the seriousness of his voice had not made it sound promising. After her performance this afternoon in the maze, she was not surprised.

Winston took Susannah's hand and led her onto the ballroom floor. He had been dancing most of the night, but he dreaded this waltz. It was high time that he be honest with Susannah, as honest as possible in any event. He owed her that much.

He did not like the wariness he read in her eyes. For the first time, Susannah Lacey looked unsure of herself, and the blame could only be laid at his feet. Neither of them spoke as he placed his right hand at her waist and pulled her close. The strains of a soft waltz began, and they swayed in time to the music. She felt too good in his arms, like she belonged there.

"I must beg your pardon for this afternoon," Susannah whispered.

Winston flushed. He had intended to apologize to her. "There is no need. I had no right to treat you as I did. I am more than ashamed."

"Please, do not be. I . . ." she hesitated, as if looking for the right phrase, "pushed you."

"Even so."

They swirled around the other dancers and fell uncomfortably quiet. There was so much he needed to say to her, and yet he hadn't a clue where to begin.

"I do know my heart," Susannah said softly.

"We knew each other only four days before I returned to war. You may think that you know me, but you do not."

"I know enough." There was a stubborn tilt to her chin.

The urge to kiss those full lips properly was nearly overwhelming. He needed a means of defense against the temptation to love her. "Did you know that I intend to leave England for India at the end of the Season?" he asked.

Shock registered in her eyes, and her footsteps faltered. "But I thought . . ."

"That I wanted to settle down here? Ponsby's words, not mine."

"I see." She was quiet for some time, as if fighting for composure. "When will you return?" she asked with a ragged voice.

"I do not know, perhaps not ever."

Her eyes clouded over, filling with tears.

His gut twisted at what he was doing to her. "I am sorry," he whispered. He pulled her closer toward him in an attempt to comfort her. The nearness of her and the way she clung to him blistered his already battered conscience. Why must he always hurt her?

They swayed and turned. Susannah thought she would die. They remained silent. There was nothing left to say, nothing she *could* say since her throat had closed up tight. He was leaving, and he did not plan on returning. In order to have him, she must leave behind everything she knew: her family, her friends, and her country. Could she do that for love? And if she could not, then did she truly love him?

She looked into Winston's guarded face and knew this was hard for him as well. Perhaps she did not know him well enough to give up everything to be with him. Why must he leave? The rumors had him a wealthy man. Could he be persuaded to stay if he loved her? Her thoughts were in such turmoil that her head ached.

"Are you all right?" he asked quietly.

"No." She tried for a light tone to her voice. "Captain, I believe you have succeeded in giving me the headache."

"Now you know how I feel," he countered with a hint of a smile softening the corners of his mouth.

She tried to match his tone. "I am, if nothing else, persistent."

"Relentless," he amended.

She smiled even though she felt sick with disappointment. She was worse off than when she first started her assault on Winston Jeffries' heart. She needed to examine her own heart more closely. Just how badly did she want this man?

*   *   *

Susannah sat in her bed drinking a cup of chocolate, contemplating her next move. She had asked to be taken straight home after her waltz with Winston, due to a headache. Olivia had been in earlier this morning to see how she fared with a worried Sheldrake hovering nearby. She had to own that she was better with the light of day.

She considered her conversation with Winston, and things simply did not add up to three. He came to London with gossip swirling about him that he was on the hunt for a wife to enjoy his newly found wealth. If he had not gone to India as he had planned when he sold out his commission, then where did his funds come from? And why did he court Caroline Dunsford if he was not enamored of her? And why would he court anyone if he were not planning to stay in England?

She must talk more to Winston when she saw him tonight at the Dunsford musicale. Caroline had invited her to play the pianoforte, which always gave her ease from her troubles. She lay back and considered what she should wear. She certainly did not feel much up to wearing white. She would much rather wear dull gray to match her mood.

She decided that a morning spent shopping might lift her spirits. She climbed out of bed and rang the bell for Botts to accompany her, since Olivia was busy with the children.

Once dressed and armed with her pin money, Susannah and Botts took the carriage to Bond Street. In no time they had managed to make several purchases, and Susannah was in relatively good humor when they headed for home. Rounding the corner, Susannah spotted Winston walking along the street. He moved at a rapid pace and entered the building of the Foreign

Office. She wondered what business he could possibly have there.

She tapped the coachman's shoulder. "Could you please pull just beyond to that side street and let me out." In another moment, she hopped down and turned to Botts. "I shall return shortly, and if you please, do not mention this to anyone."

Her maid nodded.

Susannah nearly ran up the steps of the building Winston had entered moments before. The entrance hall was large, but she could not tell where he had gone. Then she saw him. He was far enough away from her not to notice her, but she stepped behind one of the large potted palms just in case. He walked with an older man, and the two appeared to know each other well. They disappeared into an office and closed the door.

After some minutes passed, Susannah came out from behind the plant. She inched close enough to the closed door to read the golden tag: LORD CASTLE-REAGH, FOREIGN SECRETARY. She stepped back bewildered.

What business did Winston have with such a lofty person? She stood pondering a moment longer, and a shiver passed down her spine. She had heard about some of Lord Castlereagh's duties. Sheldrake told them of a debate in Parliament last year concerning the funds required by the Foreign Office for spying activities. The expense was indeed considerable.

Slowly, she exited the building and returned to her waiting carriage, almost wishing she had not followed him. Something was not quite right. Perhaps Winston was something other than what he portrayed. *"There are things I have done."* His words, excuses she thought at the time, echoed through her mind, and she suddenly felt ill with dread.

"Sweet Winston, what has happened to you," she whispered before she climbed into the carriage.

Winston entered Dunsford House. The musicale was a large gathering of guests, more than he had expected. He did not know if a crowd would make things easier for him or not. He had some extensive searching to do. Tonight he must slip away during the performances.

He had not slept well last night, yet again. He woke several times, but the last dream kept him from even attempting to sleep. He had been dripping with sweat when he awoke. The dream had been so vivid and real, that he had had to pour himself a glass of brandy to calm his shaking. The worst part of it was that Susannah had made her way into his nightmares, viewing him from afar in horror, as he carried out his orders. It made him sick to remember the look upon her beautiful face. He confronted not only his past in his dreams, but now, after last night, the fear of his future—a future where Susannah knew what he was capable of and afraid of him because of it.

He looked down at his left hand with its jagged scar. He rubbed it, wishing to erase the memory that went with it. The mottled flesh was a permanent stamp upon his conscience, and he would carry it always as a reminder of what he had done.

"Ah, Captain." Ponsby had come up from behind him.

"Ponsby."

"You look terrible."

"Thank you, nice to see you, too."

"Did you stay late at White's and drink the place empty?"

"No." After Almack's, Winston and Ponsby had spent a few hours at White's playing whist and telling tales. "Just a bit of trouble sleeping."

Ponsby looked concerned. "I expect that comes with the duty, eh?"

"Yes."

"And it cannot help that Miss Dunsford is a most agreeable young lady."

Winston sighed. "No, it does not."

Ponsby had no advice to offer other than a nod that Winston took for understanding. "Come, let us join our ladies," Ponsby said.

Winston saw Susannah immediately. She wore a gown made of peach muslin and lace. Winston thought she looked good enough to eat. Her hair was left unadorned, and it curled about her head like a fluffy cloud. She thumbed through sheet music. As if sensing him, she looked up and smiled.

Miss Dunsford addressed the guests, and a hush settled over the formal drawing room. Winston was careful to sit with Ponsby in the back row, so that he could leave unnoticed. Susannah was the first to perform. He watched, fascinated when she sat down calmly behind the pianoforte. She began to play. Her focus was completely on the sheet music as her fingers floated across keys. Divine music from the works of Beethoven, Bach, and Handel issued forth from her efforts. Winston closed his eyes as he listened. He could not leave just yet.

She played three pieces before he made himself slip silently out into the hallway. His plan was to search Lord Dunsford's study. Quietly, he opened the door and stepped inside. The room was dark but for the glow of dying embers from a banked fire. Taking a small candle from his coat pocket, he stooped near the fireplace and touched the candle's wick to a red coal until it lit to a flame. He looked about the room for a holder and grabbed a small cut-crystal goblet to steady the light.

He canvassed the room. He felt along the walls and behind paintings for safes. None were found. He felt along the mantel and bookcases for any levers or switches that would open to a secret hiding place. Again, there was nothing. Winston looked at the desk and hesitated. It would take considerable time to go through the piles of papers. Lord Dunsford was not an organized man. Would Dunsford notice if anything was left amiss? Winston sat down and began shuffling through each stack.

"What are you doing?"

Winston looked up quickly, his heart in his throat. It was Susannah. He breathed a little easier, but not by much.

"What are you doing in here?" she asked again.

"I could ask the same of you," he stalled.

"I came to find you."

"Why?" He did not like the accusing expression upon her face.

"Because, I want to know why you are going through Lord Dunsford's things." Her voice turned shrill.

"Susannah," he stood and reached out to her, in an attempt to calm her. She looked about the room, her gaze resting on the candle. His actions were obvious.

She spread her hands wide and looked shaken to the core. "Does this have anything to do with your meeting with Lord Castlereagh this morning?"

He tried not to show his surprise. She must have

followed him. "This is nothing that you need concern yourself with. Return to the drawing room and forget that you saw me."

She kept him pinned with a steely-blue gaze he never expected from her. "You know that I cannot," she whispered. "What am I to do or say to Caroline?"

Winston fingered his chin thoughtfully. He must tread delicately. "This has everything to do with my meeting with Lord Castlereagh this morning."

"Are you still part of the military or did you sell out?"

"No. I am part of the Secret Service. I report directly to Lord Castlereagh."

"What for? The war is over." Her eyes were round as saucers, and he could read fear in them. Just as in his dream, he thought bitterly.

"Because, there is still information out there that must be gathered."

"And you believe you will find this information here? From Lord Dunsford?"

"Yes," he said quietly. "We must leave before we are found."

She stood at the doorway quietly as he hurried to right everything back the way it had originally been. He blew out his candle, trimmed the wick by pinching it off, and then placed it back into his pocket. He rubbed the glass with his handkerchief and returned it next to the decanter of brandy. All this was done quickly and silently while Susannah looked on with wide eyes.

"What are you looking for?" Susannah asked.

"We cannot talk about this here. I do not wish to be seen together like this. You must return to the drawing room, and I will meet you there."

"But . . ."

He grabbed hold of her cold hands and chaffed them roughly. "Go now, my dear." Winston leaned close to her and murmured, "Be brave and put on a smile for me." He tipped her chin up with his finger. "Are you all right?"

"Give me a moment to understand all this."

"That's something I don't have, but I can give you this." He placed his lips lightly upon hers for a feather of a kiss. Her eyes closed briefly then opened. "Please, just trust me and go," he said.

Susannah leaned against the closed door to catch her breath. Her fear had lessened but her nerves still trembled and her knees felt weak. Winston was a *spy*! But he was spying upon her dearest friend's father! Her head felt light, and her stomach churned. How could she possibly face Caroline? What could her father have done to raise the attention of the Foreign Office so that they sent Winston to investigate?

It dawned on her that Winston's spying was the reason for his courtship of Caroline. That realization made her sick.

"There are things I have done."

She could have wept at the implications of Winston's words. She made her way back to the drawing room, where she took her seat next to Caroline. It took all of her resolve to act normally, but she could not meet Caroline's eyes.

"Are you all right, dear? You look pale."

Susannah took a deep breath. "I am fine. I simply needed a breath of air is all."

"It is rather warm in here. Susannah, do tell me, what scheme should we cook up this time to ensnare our gentlemen?" Caroline whispered with a slight giggle.

Scheme indeed! If Caroline only knew! But she

couldn't, not ever. For all she knew, Winston's life might depend upon utmost secrecy. Susannah shivered despite the heat of the room. "I shall have to think on it."

She turned and looked at the double doors opened wide as Winston entered. He nodded toward her and took his seat next to Lord Ponsby. Dear Heavens! What if Lord Ponsby was a spy, too? She frantically considered that possibility, but decided that he could not be, not when he was in line for an earldom.

Her nerves were decidedly pulled as song after song went on for an eternity. There was nothing for her to do, but wait. Finally, Caroline led the guests to the dining room for refreshments. Susannah remained seated but her gaze strayed to Winston as he approached.

"Are you all right?" he asked when he took a seat next to her.

"Not quite." She looked about them. The room had a soft glow from the candlelight. Susannah felt like she was in a dream, but her pounding head told her it was entirely too real. Only a few guests lingered five rows in front of them, but she knew she needed to remain calm lest they notice her agitation. She looked at Winston then down at her hands in her lap.

"I beg your pardon for distressing you. Perhaps now you understand why I attempted to court your friend, Miss Dunsford."

"I must say such a plan is entirely despicable. You asked her father permission to pay your addresses to her. What if she had fallen in love with you? What then?"

"It would have made my mission a whole lot easier," he said with dull humor.

"It is not in the least humorous," she said with a

hiss. "It is simply horrible. Is *this* the reason I never heard from you after Toulouse?"

He looked away. "Yes."

"And is this why you must go to India?" Somehow she could not imagine being married to a spy. What kind of things had he done to get the information that had been required of him? If he were capable of courting a young lady to the point of engagement, what else would he do to get what he needed? A chill raced up her spine at the possibilities.

"There are things I have done."

His expression was troubled. "Susannah, we cannot talk of this here. There are too many people who may overhear us. Perhaps we could meet in the morning, a ride in Hyde Park at, say, nine o'clock."

Reluctantly, she agreed. Winston had been right. She truly did not know him at all, and that scared her.

"I must insist that you not mention any of this to anyone. Is that clear?"

She had never seen him look so fierce before. She would not dare disobey him.

"Not to Lord Sheldrake, your sister, and especially not to Miss Dunsford." His voice was a mere whisper, but the steely strength of it broached no argument. "I will explain what I can to you tomorrow. For now rest assured that all is fine and normal."

"Fine, yes." She nodded her head then added, "I suggest that you ask my aunt's permission to ride tomorrow."

He stood and offered his arm. "Very well. Would you like some refreshments?"

She took his arm and walked with him in silence to the dining room. She had never longed for a glass of ratafia more than she did just then.

*   *   *

Caroline felt like she would scream with frustration. Lord Ponsby was positively ignoring her! She felt tears building up behind her eyes, and she blinked furiously. She was not about to break down in front of all these guests.

She should have kissed him in the maze at Burlington House when she had had the chance. She had been completely truthful when she told him she had never received a better compliment than the one he had given her. His words had gone straight to her heart, and she was utterly lost. She guessed that he did not give such flattery often. He was neither a flirt nor did he play fast and loose with a young lady's affections. So why had he drawn back from her? She had given him every possible indication that she would welcome his advances. And now he ignored her. Did he think her a featherbrain? He must have changed his mind, and that is what bothered her. What on earth did she do to make Lord Ponsby change his mind?

Chapter Nine

*W*inston paced the stable floor while he waited for his horse to be saddled. How much should he tell Susannah? Now that his mission was compromised, there was no use in keeping Susannah in the dark. But should he consider asking her assistance? Her access to Dunsford House could very well be the key to success. He highly doubted that Susannah would be placed in any danger. All of his communications with Lord Castlereagh led him to understand that there was no real network of sympathizers. Dunsford worked alone or with one or two other noblemen. Besides, he could keep her safe.

The other issue that nagged at his conscience was that his relationship with Susannah was about to change. If he used her to help him uncover the letter, it would require that he spend a considerable amount of time in her presence. He would have to train her to search properly, and they would meet regularly to report their progress. It would be near impossible to keep his feelings for her in check.

His horse was ready. He mounted the gelding and sped off at a canter. The day was cool but thankfully dry. As he rode the few blocks to Lord Sheldrake's town house, Winston realized that Lord Sheldrake could prove to be a problem as well. If he brought Susannah under his wing to spy for him, it would have every appearance of courtship. Susannah's brother-in-law had basically warned him to stay away from her if his intentions were not serious. Spying with Susannah was bound to put him in a precarious situation. But he saw no other way.

He released his breath with a heavy sigh. He was truly in the suds this time. If required to declare his intentions toward Susannah Lacey, he could only assure Lord Sheldrake that they were honorable, which might mean a possible offer of marriage. If he called on Susannah without declaring his intentions, he felt quite certain he and Lord Sheldrake would eventually have words. Either way he looked at it, the result would be the same. He might be required to offer for Susannah.

His heart lurched with hope at the thought, only to plummet back to reality. He'd have to tell Susannah about the cause of his nightmares. He'd not let her accept him without knowing everything about him. That alone might lead her to cry off. Considering that he had given his word to go to India regardless, he felt fairly confident that Susannah would not go. He doubted that she could leave behind everything she knew and loved just to be with him. That gave him considerable confidence in securing her help. As perfect as Miss Susannah Lacey was, she feared the unfamiliar.

He slowed his horse to a trot as he approached Grosvenor Square, where the Sheldrake residence stood. He felt oddly assured of what he must do as he dismounted and tied his horse to the front post. He ran up the steps and pounded on the door with the heavy brass knocker.

"I am Captain Jeffries, here to call upon Miss Lacey," he said to the butler.

"Miss Susannah is expecting you. Come this way to the breakfast room." Winston followed the austere fellow down the hall to a room filled with laughter.

"Captain Jeffries, do come in," Lady Sheldrake said. "Have you had breakfast?"

"Yes." He had eaten a couple of muffins with coffee before he left.

"Very well. Susannah has gone to fetch her bonnet. Do sit down and make yourself comfortable." Lady Sheldrake gestured toward a vacant chair next to her aunt.

He felt her aunt's wary gaze as he took a seat. He was grateful that he did not have to face Lord Sheldrake this morning. "Good morning, Miss Wilts," he said to her.

"Captain. How are you today?"

"Quite well, and you?"

"I am hale and hearty and quite fit." There was an edge to her voice. It appeared that every one of Susannah's family were angry with him. He should not really blame them. He looked at Lady Sheldrake, who had always treated him with utmost kindness. Perhaps she was the only one who had forgiven him for hurting Susannah.

"Good morning, Captain Jeffries." Susannah entered. He could have sworn that the room brightened by her smile. She wore a deep blue riding habit that fit her delectable form nicely. Her golden curls bobbed underneath a bonnet made of the same stuff. Winston was hard-pressed not to stare. She looked so beautiful.

"Good morning," he finally said. He noticed that Lady Sheldrake tried to hide a knowing smile behind her copy of the *Morning Post*. Miss Wilts nodded with what looked faintly like approval. "Shall we go?" he asked as he stood.

"Yes," Susannah agreed.

"I shall return your niece within two hours," Winston said to Miss Wilts.

"Thank you, Captain." Lady Sheldrake and her aunt chimed in unison.

He nodded to both the ladies and left with Susannah upon his arm.

"How did you sleep?" he whispered when they were halfway down the hall.

"Better than you, it appears."

He shrugged. He had been restless again last night. "I do not sleep well," he explained.

She nodded but said nothing. They exited the front door, and the groom stood holding the reins of a mare the color of gray skies. Susannah stepped lightly into the sidesaddle with the groom's help.

Winston settled onto his gelding. "Let us ride first, and then we can talk."

They trotted toward Hyde Park and made their way to within sight of the sandy track known as Rotten Row. There were other riders present, but not many, so Winston asked, "Shall we let them stretch their legs?"

Susannah smiled in response and nodded before she kicked her mare into an easy canter. He lagged behind just to watch her. He remembered that she had ridden well at Sheldrake Hall, but she had improved on her skill. She and the mare were well matched. Her horse responded to each command without hesitation, and the two of them blazed a fast trail toward the track.

He urged his gelding forward, and the high-strung fellow darted with a jump into a full gallop. Winston enjoyed the freedom of moving at near breakneck speed. He loved the feel of a good horse beneath him. It had been ages since he had ridden simply for the pure enjoyment of it.

He overtook Susannah and passed her with a grin. He'd race with her if she dared. She was up to the challenge and urged her mare forward. They took the track with amazing speed to the delight of the other riders who stopped to watch them fly once, twice, then a third time around. Susannah reined back and fell out of a gallop into a trot.

He did the same. He was pleased to see that she smiled when she brought her horse alongside of his.

"You ride well," she said.

"I was thinking the same of you."

"I did not wish to push her too hard." She patted her mare's neck.

Winston nodded. The horse did look a bit winded.

"She's not nearly as fast or in as good a shape as the gelding you have there. Where did you get him?"

"He is not mine. He belongs to Ponsby. He gave him to me for the time being to test his meddle."

"You ride as if you were born to a saddle, but, then, I suppose a captain in the cavalry would be expected to have such expertise."

Winston nodded his agreement. "When my father bought my commission, he agreed that the cavalry would be the best place for me. I have ridden all my life."

"Your father was a baronet was he not?"

"Yes, and my brother inherited his title and estate not long after I entered the military." They now walked their horses away from the track, but rode side by side to let the animals cool down.

"When did you last see your brother?" Susannah asked.

He knew she was making small talk, and he wondered if she wished to avoid the reason they had met this morning.

"Before I came to London." He absently stroked the gelding between his ears.

"Is he well?"

"As well as he can be." When she looked confused, Winston explained. "Brian, my brother, lost his arm in a farming accident a few years ago. His elbow was crushed, and there was no setting of the bone and so it had to come off. His wife has had trouble with it ever since. She can hardly stand to be near him."

"I am sorry."

"Yes, well, the parson says for better or for worse, but I am afraid many ladies cannot handle the *worse*." He wondered if Susannah could handle his own worse actions of his past.

"That is not quite fair, Winston. How do you know that it is not your brother who has changed toward his wife? Perhaps he will not allow her to get near him? Perhaps he fears her rejection more than she cares about his injury."

He had never considered that scenario. He had only known there was tension between the two of them and that the whole situation caused his brother pain.

When he remained silent, Susannah wasted no time. "Men can be very stubborn," she said. "They do not always recognize the strength of a woman's love." She looked pointedly at him. Was she trying to tell him that she loved him? She hardly knew him.

"I suppose," he finally said as he gathered up his reins. "Come let us find a place where we can sit down." He led them to an expanse of open lawn where one large tree stood proud, casting shade from the morning sun that peeped out from behind the gray clouds. There was no one nearby save for the other riders making their way through the park at a leisurely pace.

He dismounted and tethered his horse to a low limb. When he turned to help Susannah, she had already slid from the saddle, which surprised him. He had expected her to wait for him to help her. She tethered the mare farther down the same low limb, and the two horses grazed peacefully on the lush grass.

Winston held out his arm to gesture for her to sit down. Susannah tripped on a tree root and tumbled. Winston moved fast. He caught her in his arms.

Susannah found herself staring into Winston's cravat. He held her in a firm embrace against his chest. The one time she did not wish to be close to him, her clumsiness forced her into his arms. She cleared her throat and looked up.

A hint of a smile tugged at the corners of his mouth. He knew she was not nearly as graceful as she should be, but it amused him rather than embarrassed him. The interesting part was that he had not let go of her.

She was sorely tempted to stay that way, but knew that she needed to discuss his current state of employ as a spy before she let her feelings for him have their way. She needed a clear head today and pulled out of his embrace.

"Are you all right?" he whispered.

"Fine," she said quickly. Too quickly. But she was nervous. She was not sure she wanted to hear what Winston had to say. What if it changed how she felt about him?

"Here." Winston pulled off his bottle-green coat and laid it down for her to sit upon.

"Will you not be chilled?" The air was brisk with a stiff breeze.

"I am fine, I assure you." His voice was rich and smooth, and he appeared relaxed as he lounged next to her as if he hadn't a care in the world. But his eyes and the darkness below them proved otherwise.

They fell into silence, and Susannah brushed her skirt several times. Winston pulled up a long blade of grass and chewed on its end.

"Winston, we are here to talk," she finally said.

"Forgive me." Winston tossed the blade of grass aside. "I do not know quite where to begin."

"What about this mission? Tell me about it."

He sighed. "It is suspected that Lord Dunsford has sympathies toward Napoleon," he said quietly.

Susannah could not keep from gasping. "But why, he is an English diplomat is he not?"

"Yes, he is, and that is why I have been assigned to search out his home for a letter. Information has been uncovered that links a couple of nobles to a plan that may have financed Napoleon's efforts to escape from Elba."

"It cannot be!"

Winston nodded.

Fear gripped her with its cold fingers clutching her heart. "Is there a threat of more war?"

"I personally do not believe so, but the Foreign Office cannot rest on assumptions. These intercepted posts have to be thoroughly investigated to ferret out any traitorous activities."

"I see." Susannah realized the enormity of the task at hand. "How does Lord Dunsford fit into this?"

"A letter was intercepted by a British officer from a French ambassador. There were names of four peers listed in code as possible sympathizers toward Napoleon. Lord Dunsford was one of the men listed."

"But you have no proof," Susannah argued.

"Correct. What I seek is a letter of appreciation signed from Napoleon himself for the support given. If I find this letter in the possession of Lord Dunsford, then treason can be assumed and the Foreign Office would have reason to take action by means of a trial."

Susannah shook her head to clear it. Poor Caroline! "Has anyone found such a letter yet?"

"So far, only one of the men listed has had such a letter." Winston looked away from her as he said it.

"What happened to him?"

"The man shot himself." Again, he pulled another blade of grass and chewed it.

Her hand flew to cover her mouth. She felt sick to think of how Caroline would fall to pieces if her father did such a thing.

"The disposition of his estate is still being considered, or so I have heard," Winston said.

This was incredibly serious. Susannah prayed that Lord Dunsford had nothing to do with sending funds to France and Napoleon's army. "What of the other three men?"

"One man died in a carriage accident over two years ago, and so it is unlikely that he actually contributed. At least the Foreign Office is leaving it alone. The other man is currently being searched by another officer."

Susannah had to own that despite her shock, she was fascinated. It was as if a scene from one of her novels had suddenly sprung to life. But this was very real and very serious. A chill took hold of her, settling deep inside. "And you have been doing this since you recovered from your saber wound at Toulouse?"

"Yes, and that is why I could not write to you," Winston said quickly.

"But if you were here in England, looking for letters . . ."

"Susannah, I have had other assignments. This is the only one where I have actually worked in England."

"I see." She looked more closely at Winston and tried to decipher just how much he had changed from the carefree captain she had met that summer. Now she understood what had turned him so serious. The evidence of his troubled sleep proved that what he did was not easy on him. She imagined that it was difficult to sleep soundly when you held a man's reputation in the balance. She was sorely tempted to ask him about those other assignments, but at the same time she feared what he might tell her.

She looked down at his hands and noticed that Winston had taken off his gloves. His left hand, the scarred one, rested flat upon the ground as he leaned on it. The hideous scar looked almost as if it had been a bite mark it was so ragged. She reached out and traced the scar with her fingertip, much to Winston's obvious displeasure. He pulled his hand back.

"Did you receive that during battle?" she asked.

He rubbed his hand then put his gloves back on silently. "No," he finally said. "I received it after."

"What happened?" She waited for him to tell her the tale, but he remained silent. It must be something too horrible to tell. She did not ask him again.

"There are things I have done."

The words he had whispered in Lord Elgin's maze haunted her. She wondered just what those *things* might be. And yet if they had been done in the name of his duty to the crown, how could she possibly fault him?

Minutes passed without either of them saying a word. Each of them watched the activity of riders trotting by.

"Susannah," he finally said quietly. His dark brown eyes were solemn. "I believe I may need your help."

"How can I help you?" she asked cautiously.

"I do not have access to Dunsford House like you do."

Her stomach felt like it had dropped out of her. He wanted her to search for the letter. That piece of paper could very well ruin her dear friend's life. She was not sure she could be a party to that. Another chill raced through her body making her shiver. She wrapped her arms about herself in an effort to still her shakes as she stared at the ground.

"You are cold," he said. "Perhaps we should walk."

She held out her hand to keep him from getting up. "No." She breathed deeply in an attempt to calm her insides. What would she do if she found the letter? How could she ever face Caroline again?

Winston placed his finger under her chin and gently forced her head up so he could search her eyes. "I know this is difficult," he whispered. "I know how fond of Miss Dunsford you have become. The faster we resolve this issue, the better it will be for everyone."

"But what if he does not keep it at Dunsford House? Or what if he has burned it?" She clasped her hands firmly together.

"I know. I have thought the same things, but the humorous thing about traitors is that they believe they are doing right. In fact, they often take pride in what they have done. A letter such as this, signed by Napoleon himself, would not be destroyed. Instead, it is a document of great value. One that is most likely kept with other things they hold dear, such as jewels and the like."

She was impressed by the conviction in his tone, but

she felt adrift, as if this were all a dream. With a sinking feeling, she knew she would agree to help him. She had fretted all night about the possibility that he would ask her. "What is it that you wish me to do?"

He reached out and took hold of her clasped hands and raised them to his lips for a brief kiss. "I need only for you to search rooms for a wall safe, or a secret hiding place, and that is all. I have made a list of the rooms that I have already been through. That should give you a start. Once you have found the most likely place to store treasures, I can take over from there. We must meet regularly to discuss our progress. And we must visit Miss Dunsford as often as we can."

"I can search when I am there on my own," she offered.

"Yes, but again, look only for hiding places and secret drawers. It is important that you leave everything exactly as you found it. You cannot alert Dunsford to what we seek." He pulled out a small folded piece of paper. "This is my list."

"I understand."

Winston checked his watch, then stood. "It is getting late," he said as he reached out his hand to help her.

"When will I see you again?" she asked.

He bent down and picked up his coat from off the ground, shook it out then put it on, shrugging into the tight-fitting garment as best as he could. "Tonight. I have been invited to dinner by Lord Sheldrake."

Susannah did not bother to mask her surprise. "You have? When?"

"Last night. Before you left the Dunsford's musicale, I asked Lord Sheldrake's permission to call upon you this morning. He is protective of you. I cannot say that I blame him."

Susannah felt her cheeks grow hot. "You will be as good as courting me." She brushed off the bits of grass from his coat and straightened his lapel. It was a completely familiar gesture, but Winston did not seem to mind.

"I know," he said. Then he smiled.

Her heart thudded. She had wanted this forever, but now she felt afraid. What if Lord Dunsford truly was a traitor? How could she feel happy about finally being with Winston if it meant harming her friend? And what of Winston? He had warned her before that she did not really know him. What would she find out about him now that she knew he was a spy?

Winston stood while Pegston adjusted his cravat. Tonight he dined with Susannah and her family. He needed to look his best.

"She must be a special lady," Pegston said.

"Who?"

"The one you are getting all gussied up for." Pegston stood back to survey the masterpiece of a cravat that he had just tied. He winked. "Perfection."

"Every time," Winston added.

Susannah was special indeed, and yet he felt nervous. All this time he had tried to keep her at a distance while she doggedly pursued him. Today he saw her determination falter, and he felt oddly disappointed. He would not have blamed her if she refused to have anything further to do with him, and he was glad that she did not. Despite her pretty words about a woman's love, he wondered if she could stand by them once she knew just what he had done.

Whistling softly, he walked the few short blocks to Susannah's home. The butler escorted him to the drawing room, but he hesitated in the entryway. He felt like an intruder upon the idyllic scene before him. They were a study of blissful family life, and he envied their carefree security.

Lord Sheldrake and his wife sat upon a divan with their infant son between them while a little girl ran about the room. Lady Evelyn and Miss Wilts played cards, and Susannah poured her heart out onto the keys of the pianoforte. Winston stood transfixed as he watched her. The butler announced him, but it took Winston a moment to divert his attention to Lord Sheldrake, who stood to welcome him.

"Good evening, Captain." Lord Sheldrake stretched out his hand.

Winston took it for a firm handshake. "Thank you for your invitation."

Susannah stopped playing and smiled shyly at him from across the room.

"Nothing elaborate. I hope you do not mind," Lord Sheldrake said. "Just a quiet evening with family."

Winston wondered if Lord Sheldrake offered a place in this family. "I am honored that you chose to include me," he said to him. Apparently he had been given a second chance to prove himself worthy of Susannah.

"Dinner will not be served for a while yet. Come and meet my children," Lord Sheldrake said. "This is little Jane, the child my wife carried the summer you met Susannah."

An auburn-haired girl of about three smiled up at him with huge green eyes like her mother's. Winston knelt down so that he could speak to her at eye level. "How do you do?"

"Are you going to marry Aunt Susannah?" she asked innocently.

"Jane!" Susannah cried. "That is not a polite question to ask."

"But you said . . ." Jane had turned defiantly toward Susannah.

"Never mind, dear," Lady Sheldrake interrupted. "I beg your pardon, Captain."

"No need," Winston said hurriedly, but he could not keep his gaze from straying to Susannah, who flushed to the roots of her hair. He wondered what she had said about him.

"And this."—Lord Sheldrake picked up his boy—"Is my son and heir, George."

Winston reached out to shake the mite's hand. "How old is he?"

"Just turned a year." Lord Sheldrake beamed with pride upon his son's fuzzy dark head.

"A regular terror, he is," Lady Evelyn chimed in as she played her next card. "And a healthy set of lungs, just like his father."

Winston walked over to the table where the two ladies played a furiously serious round of piquet. "Good evening, Lady Evelyn and Miss Wilts. Who has the lead?"

"Evelyn does," Miss Wilts answered, her attention on her cards.

"Very well, do proceed. I do not wish to distract you." He took a seat near Susannah. "This is very pleasant," he whispered.

"All the more so since you are here." She looked away quickly.

"I thank you." He shifted awkwardly. Susannah was not completely at ease with him. Although she tried to hide it, she seemed wary of him.

The meal was wonderful, the company relaxed and

accepting of him. He had laughed several times at stories told of Susannah and her sister when they were young. The deep love and respect this family had for one another was a tangible thing that Winston soaked in like a dry sponge.

He did not even mind Lord Sheldrake's scrutiny when the ladies left them to their port. How could Susannah ever leave her family and go to India? The thought sobered him, yet he found himself explaining his future plans to Lord Sheldrake.

"This partnership you have entered into with Lord Ponsby sounds like a good prospect." Lord Sheldrake swished his port in his glass.

"Despite what you may have heard, I am not so very plump in the pockets. I have only a military income of sorts," Winston said.

Lord Sheldrake digested the information and nodded. "Please understand the reason that I asked you to dine with us, Captain. I must know what your intentions are toward Susannah. I will not see her hurt again."

Winston braced himself. "I understand."

"I do not think you do. Every night I had to listen to that girl's sobs after she read that you fell at Toulouse. When we heard nothing from you, I sought information through every connection I had with no success. You were not listed among the dead or the deserted, yet no one knew what had happened to you. Just what have you been up to?"

"I am not at liberty to say, my lord." Winston knew he was on dangerous ground. Based on what Lord Sheldrake had just told him, by refusing to answer, he hinted at what he was.

Lord Sheldrake narrowed his eyes and looked as if he wanted to say more but thought better of it.

Winston owed the man an explanation. "Lord Sheldrake." He chose his words carefully. "I have only honorable intentions toward Susannah. I do not wish to hurt her for the world, but I cannot promise that she will not suffer heartbreak. I have given my word as a gentleman to go to India. It is quite possible that Susannah will not wish to join me. Even so, I must leave."

"I understand." Lord Sheldrake seemed satisfied and let the matter drop. "Well, then." He stood. "Let us join the ladies, shall we?"

Chapter Ten

"*I* need you to come with us," Winston said as he sat down in Ponsby's study.

"It's rather uncomfortable for me." Ponsby took a sip of his tea.

"Why?"

"First you are courting Caro, I mean Miss Dunsford, and now all of a sudden I am supposed to step in and keep her busy for you?"

"You have already done so."

"Yes, but that was before . . ." Ponsby broke off in mid-sentence.

"Before what?" Winston helped himself to a biscuit. Ponsby would not look at him.

"The deuce, Ponsby! You have feelings for Miss Dunsford!" They were perfect for each other, save that Miss Dunsford's father might be a traitor to the crown. A surge of anger filled him. How many lives need be ruined because of one man's misplaced allegiances!

"Does it show?" he asked.

"Not really." Winston had not noticed but then his mind had been occupied elsewhere most of the time. "She is a taking young woman and not ignorant of you, I might add."

"I know. She would make an excellent countess and

yet . . ." Ponsby refilled his cup. "What is it that you search for?"

Winston hesitated.

Ponsby held up his hand. "Never mind. Perhaps it is better that I do not know."

Winston nodded. He was not about to bring up the subject of engaging Susannah's help. The less the subject was discussed, the better for everyone involved. "Will you join us when we call upon Miss Dunsford later today?"

"I will. Despite my reservations, I find that it is difficult to stay away."

Winston knew exactly how Ponsby felt. "What will you do?"

"Do? There is nothing I can do. I shall simply have to wait until you are finished with your cursed assignment."

Winston felt a tremendous weight upon his conscience. His assignment had become too entangled. Winston wanted his post in India more than anything, but the prospect of success at the cost of people he cared about was appalling. If he succeeded in finding that letter, Miss Dunsford would be ruined and Ponsby would never offer for her.

"We shall take the closed carriage," Ponsby finally muttered. "It looks like rain."

"Indeed." Winston headed for the door but stopped. He turned toward Ponsby. "I am sorry about all this, old boy. I wish to God that it was different."

"I know that you do," Ponsby said with a slight smile. "But we are men of duty are we not? You protect the crown and I protect my heritage. Each of us has to live by a code that is larger than what our hearts feel. Knowing this is difficult for you assures me that you have not lost your soul."

Winston was moved more than he cared to admit. No matter what happened with Lord Dunsford, Winston owed Ponsby for his help. It was an unspoken debt; one that Ponsby would never call in but Winston was determined to pay somehow.

Susannah waited by the front window. The day was dreary with steady rain that showed no signs of letting up. She watched Lord Ponsby's crested carriage slow as it neared the curb. She ran to the foyer to fetch her large black umbrella. "I shall return in a couple of hours," she called out to her aunt. "I am joining Miss Dunsford for tea."

Aunt Agatha peeked her head around the door from the front parlor. "Very well, dear. Enjoy yourself."

"Yes, aunt." Susannah leaned forward and gave her a kiss upon the cheek.

"Things have turned a bit with your young captain, have they not?" her aunt asked with a shrewd look.

"Perhaps." Susannah was not about to discuss it now.

"Do you think him worth the trouble?" she asked.

That was a question she had recently asked herself. Winston was a spy. There was much she did not know or understand about him. The kiss they shared in Lord Elgin's maze was evidence that what she thought she wanted had proved to be less than what she expected. Although she cared deeply for Winston, she could not be sure that following him to India was the right thing to do. Her determination had faltered, and now she felt unsure. "I will know that soon enough," Susannah said as she rushed out of the door.

The rain was cold and caused her to shiver even with the benefit of her large umbrella. Lord Ponsby's tiger stepped down and opened the door for her. She climbed in carefully, placing the closed umbrella upon the floor.

"We could have escorted you," Lord Ponsby protested.

Susannah waved her hand in dismissal as she sat down next to Winston. "I watched for your carriage. There was no sense in having either of you soaked to the skin."

Winston smiled when she glanced at him. "Very practical," he said.

"Of course, I am from the country where practicality is of utmost importance." She leaned back in her seat, and they were off. In moments they pulled up close to the front door of Dunsford House. Lord Ponsby bounded out of the door before Susannah could offer her umbrella as a shield. She turned to Winston. "You can share with me."

"Thank you," he said softly.

An unbidden tremor shook her, but it was not due to the cold. Winston got out and used the umbrella to shield her as best he could. "This rain is cursed. I vow I'll not miss this weather," Winston mumbled. He draped his arm around her and pulled her close to huddle under the umbrella.

His warmth immediately enveloped Susannah, and she suddenly worried if she could actually place one foot in front of the other without tripping. She felt an insane urge to remain within his embrace for an eternity. Seeking something intelligent to say, Susannah countered his complaint. "But the rain keeps the grass green," she said. "How much lush green can be found in your India?"

"The sun always shines warmly. For that I will gladly trade green grass."

"Winston," Susannah said, feeling irritable. There was no keeping him in England, not now or ever. That fact left her with a hollow feeling. "I think your blood has thinned."

"I suppose it has," he said with a chuckle.

They made their way up the slippery rain-soaked steps and entered the large anteroom where Caroline helped the butler take their sodden outer garments.

"Do come in and get warm before the fire. I vow this is the most horrid of days," Caroline said.

"You sound like Captain Jeffries." Susannah followed Caroline into the hall.

Winston stepped close behind her. With his lips nearly touching her ear, he whispered, "When I leave the drawing room, make up an excuse and follow me. I will meet you in the room where you repaired your hem."

She nodded and took a deep breath. Her education was about to begin. Looking at the back of Caroline, she reverently hoped that there was no letter to be found. She glanced at Winston, wondering how he could remain so calm when she felt like a shaking leaf. But amid her fear, she felt a stirring of excitement, an unholy thrill.

When they entered the drawing room, they took their usual places, except this time, Lord Ponsby stood close to the fireplace. The four of them chatted about the latest gossip, and then the conversation lagged.

"I beg your pardon," Winston said just before he sneezed. And then he sneezed again. "I believe I may seek out your cook one more time for a draught."

Caroline leaned back, not wishing to catch whatever she thought Winston may have. "Goodness, yes. You do appear tired, Captain. My abigail is abed this very day due to her sniffles. Perhaps you, too, should take to your bed once you go home."

Susannah looked at Winston to see how he reacted.

"Miss Dunsford, you are quite right. But for now, I shall seek out your cook. I will return shortly," he said with a pointed look in Susannah's direction.

That was the sign.

She searched her mind for an excuse. She realized that it mattered not what she said. Caroline and Lord Ponsby kept looking at one another, and Susannah might as well have been a spider in the corner, for all the attention they paid her. "Uhmmm," she stammered. "I think I shall go with Captain Jeffries."

Caroline nodded in her direction, but neither she nor Lord Ponsby appeared to have heard her. She left the room and dashed down the hallway. Looking in each direction to be sure no one saw her, she slipped into the small sitting room as instructed by Winston.

The door opened and Winston looked up in time to see Susannah enter. She leaned upon the closed door, and her chest heaved as she breathed heavily. Her eyes sparkled with excitement, and Winston wondered when she had looked better. "Are you ready for your first lesson?" he asked. His blood warmed considerably as he watched her.

"Yes," she said breathlessly. "This is very much like something from a Mrs. Radcliff novel."

"Not quite," Winston said, amused. "You will soon find that it becomes tedious." He held out his hand to her. She took it easily, their fingers twining together. "When you enter a room, you must memorize exactly how it was when you first entered. That is how you must leave it."

Susannah nodded, her expression eager.

"Then, turn and scan the walls. Mentally plan where to start and end, so that you may come back to it, should you be interrupted. Always search the same way, use the same routine. It will make it easier to remember where you left off, should you need to return." He glanced at her and noted that she listened carefully. He walked toward the room's entrance. "I usually start at the door and work clockwise.

"And this," he said as he stooped down, "is how I search for hidden safes and places to hide things." He brushed his hands along the floor, then up the molding onto the wall. He stood, feeling along the wall the whole way until he could not reach any farther. He moved and repeated the same process only in reverse.

"My goodness," Susannah whispered. "It *is* tedious work."

"It is that." He held out his hand to her. "Come, let me see you give it a go."

He noted that her cheeks colored slightly as she knelt to feel along the floorboards and molding just as he had demonstrated. She continued to search the wall, her slender fingers feeling for any change in the surface. "Very good. You are fast."

She turned to look at him, but her hands continued to work their way over the wall. She connected with a mirror that tilted dangerously beneath her touch. He moved quickly. He trapped her between his arms as he grabbed hold of each side of the mirror to steady it before it crashed upon her.

She gasped and turned around only to flatten herself against the glass.

"I did not want this to fall," he explained thickly. He realized how close they were. The mirror was heavy. He could not let go without losing his grip upon it. Awkwardly, he anchored the mirror against its hook, and it held fast when he tested it. He let go only to place his hands upon the wall on either side of Susannah, keeping her trapped.

He could feel her breath upon his neck, and he looked down. It was a mistake. She gazed up at him with wide eyes of bright blue. She was the magnet and he was steel.

"Thank you for catching that," she said with a soft breathy voice. "If you have not already noticed, I am a bit clumsy at times."

He thought of how she had tripped and fallen in her drawing room when he first called upon her. It was an endearing quirk, but could prove dangerously inconvenient when stealth was critical. "You are most welcome." He stepped closer, allowing his chest to brush against hers. "But you must be more careful. Any sound can alert someone of your presence."

Susannah did not mistake the warning Winston gave her, and she shivered. Was he using his imposing physique to drive that warning home so that she would remember to be cautious, or did he simply want to be near her? She could not distinguish his reasons for practically standing upon her toes. Perhaps it was a bit of both.

She looked into his eyes, and still he did not move away from her. She leaned against the mirror that had almost fallen on her, deliciously trapped by his arms as he braced them on either side of her. Her heart pounded wildly. She felt fear and desire mix into a heady blend of need. She stood her ground, waiting for Winston's next move. She stared into his eyes as if she could read into the depth of his soul.

She trembled when she realized that her Winston was not the dashing captain she had idolized for three years. Before her stood a battle-trained man of war who had no doubt committed fearless acts in the line of duty to his country.

"There are things I have done."

His words played through her mind. She looked at him as if seeing him for what he was, unclouded by the memories she cherished from the time she was sixteen. The severity of the strength she could feel in him frightened her slightly. She also knew that he would keep her safe. She felt protected.

Suddenly overwhelmed, she placed both her hands upon his chest to push him away. "Winston, what are you doing to me?"

He blinked, realizing the position in which he had her. "I beg your pardon." He let his arms slide down to his sides, but he did not back away from her. "I merely . . ." He stopped and looked away. "I can easily get lost in your eyes."

"What do you find when you look there?" she asked softly.

"A safe place." He brought both her hands to his lips for a sweet kiss that left her weak in the knees.

"Come," he said. "We had best return, or Miss Dunsford may send someone to look for us. Besides, we have yet to visit Cook for her draught."

Susannah nodded, but her insides were weak indeed. Their relationship had definitely changed, only she did not know into what. He did not treat her as a suitor would, but then how many young men of her acquaintance were spies? Spies that asked for her help in accomplishing their mission, no less. He did not treat her merely as a friend either, since he desired her. Still, he held back from her. When she got too close, he pulled back as if he wished to pull a shutter down on what he felt for her. If she intended to have him, she still had work to do. "Very well, then, let us go to Cook," Susannah agreed.

The clock ticking upon the wall seemed excruciatingly loud to Lord Ponsby. He sat near the fire, across the room from Caroline, who would not look at him. Since Winston and Susannah had left, they had spoken only of the unusually cold spring weather and the latest society gossip. And now they were awkwardly silent once again. She nervously brushed her gown, clasped her hands, and placed them firmly in her lap. She looked up at him, and he found that he could not look away.

They were completely alone. Caroline's abigail was abed with a cold. Lord Dunsford was away from the house, which Lord Ponsby had learned was a common occurrence. Caroline sat stiffly, her chin held high, and he realized that this was the cool and confident front she portrayed to the *ton*. Before him sat the Ice Princess, but there was a small crack in the ice of her dark eyes. She was alone far too often. By blocking her out and staying away from her, he had hurt her.

"Would you care for tea, Lord Ponsby?" she asked. "I can have it brought straight away. You must still be chilled from the rain."

It was her carefully controlled voice that chilled him. "Caroline," he said, "I am sorry."

She cocked her head, trying to understand why he begged her forgiveness. "Whatever for, my lord?" Still that calm and distant voice, as if she had no emotions.

He got up and crossed the floor in a trice to kneel before her. She jerked back in her chair unsure of his presence, his nearness. He took hold of both her hands to keep her seated. "I have treated you unfairly.

The last time I was here, I . . ." he broke off when he noticed a tiny tear escape from her eye to run down her cheek.

He could stand it no longer; he had to kiss her.

Caroline could hardly believe what was happening. No sooner did Lord Ponsby's lips connect with hers, than they heard the sounds of Winston and Susannah in the hallway. Lord Ponsby pulled back quickly as the two entered the room.

Winston returned with Susannah after being gone close to half of an hour, but neither Miss Dunsford nor Ponsby appeared to have missed them.

"I have two more," Winston said as he raised his bottles high. The tension in the room was so thick he could have stabbed it with a sword. Ponsby looked dashed uncomfortable, and Miss Dunsford appeared to be struggling with her composure as well. Either they have quarreled or kissed, Winston mused.

He raised his eyebrow at Ponsby in an effort to inquire, but the young lord merely shook his head slightly and gazed into the fire.

Susannah chattered gaily at Miss Dunsford about what seemed to Winston as frivolous nonsense. But she cast quick glances toward Ponsby while she spoke. She sensed something was amiss and was doing her best to smooth over the awkward feeling that hung in the air.

"Care for a game of cards?" Winston asked Ponsby.

"A few short hands, and then we had best be on our way."

"Agreed," Winston said as he pulled a deck from out of a gilt box sitting upon a small table. He dealt the cards, but his attention strayed to Susannah.

He did not know what had come over him earlier.

He was not sure what he had been trying to prove by boxing her in against that bloody mirror. He wanted her, and yet he was not sure if he could have her. With Susannah Lacey came a cost that could not be considered only in pounds and guineas.

She did not wish to leave England. She was adamant, in fact, about staying here. She would no doubt test him about his past. She would never let him go on this way, having nightmares and restless nights. She promised safety from what ailed him, yet he feared her reaction to what caused them. If finding healing from his guilt meant losing her respect and possible love, then he would rather keep his sleepless nights.

Caroline showed her guests out. She had done her best to explain what had happened to Susannah while the men had played cards. It was difficult because it sounded so terribly odd. Lord Ponsby had apologized for ignoring her, and then he had kissed her. They had not had any time to enjoy the kiss, but at least it was a start.

"Do take care not to catch cold," she said before Susannah and Winston dashed out into the pouring rain under the umbrella they shared. She was immensely happy to see that her dearest friend was making progress with her captain.

Lord Ponsby hesitated. He had his gloves in hand, but did not appear to be in a hurry to leave. He kept looking shamefaced as he cast awkward glances toward her butler.

"Duncan," Caroline said to the trusted servant. "If we could have a moment in private, please."

"Madam." The butler bowed stiffly with obvious disapproval, then departed.

"Thank you," Lord Ponsby said. He clasped her

hands once again. "Caroline. I must beg your forgiveness yet again."

"Why?"

"I have acted in a forward manner. I had no right to make you, uncomfortable."

She nearly groaned with frustration. First he ignored her, then he kissed her and is sorry for it? "My lord," she began. "Please do not say another word. Your kiss was merely a fleeting thing." She looked down at her shoes, feeling completely vulnerable. She gathered her courage. She met his gaze squarely and said, "Your kiss was far from uncomfortable. Incomplete is more appropriate, I think."

She smiled when she saw the surprise on his face. She had firmly encouraged his suit.

His eyes clouded over. "I understand." He was gone out into the rain before she could say anything more.

Chapter Eleven

*T*wo weeks passed, and Susannah felt worse than ever. It was increasingly difficult to look Caroline in the eye, and she was running out of excuses to steal away. Susannah and Winston had effectively searched every room with the exception of Lord Dunsford's private apartments, which were kept locked. They had not found a safe.

One evening, Susannah had stayed over night at Dunsford House due to a ball she had attended with Caroline. Even in the wee hours, Susannah was unable to find a way to enter Lord Dunsford's rooms. The safe and the letter had to be there—if such a letter existed.

Invited to a dinner party held at Dunsford House, Winston and Susannah planned to gain entry into Lord Dunsford's rooms while Caroline and her father were busy with their guests. Lord Ponsby promised to do what he could to keep Caroline's attention away from them.

Susannah looked in the mirror and was satisfied at her reflection. She had carefully chosen a gown of white muslin that was comfortable. She needed freedom of movement. Winston could not afford a partner who could barely raise her hands.

The time they had spent together these last two weeks had been filled with the details of searches. Winston demonstrated amazing patience as each progress report they shared failed to hint at where Lord Dunsford might hide a letter from Napoleon. She admired the iron control he kept on himself. He rushed nothing. He maintained a calm exterior as he thoroughly searched even some of the rooms Susannah had gone over. He missed nothing.

Their relationship had changed yet again. Instead of a fiery romance she had once hoped for, a strong friendship had bloomed. With that came a solid trust in one another. The problem was that Susannah was not satisfied with mere friendship. She felt like she was falling in love with Winston all over again, and it made her edgy because she still knew so little about what had happened to him. He had changed, but she did not know why. She wanted him, but she was afraid to leave all that she knew to follow him. The other problem was that Winston had not given her any indication that he wanted her to follow him. He remained guarded whenever she got too close.

Tonight, she decided, she would wear the ruby stickpin he had given her three years ago. She cherished their friendship, but it was not enough. It was time to make Winston Jeffries open up to her and let her come inside. The only way she knew how to trigger such a conversation was to remind him of their past.

After a brief carriage ride, Susannah entered Dunsford House on the arm of Lady Evelyn. Sheldrake and Olivia stepped in after them. Aunt Agatha had decided to stay behind. Her aunt had just borrowed the latest Mrs. Radcliffe novel from the lending library and would no doubt stay up half the night reading it.

"Susannah, good evening!" Caroline hugged her

lightly. It had been two days since last they had seen each other.

Riddled with guilt, Susannah returned the embrace. "You look lovely," she said. Caroline had made a grand departure from her usual rose and pink, to the latest shade of violet that made her eyes look so dark, they could have been black.

"Do you like it?" Caroline asked as she twirled.

"Very much. The color is wonderful on you." Susannah leaned forward and lowered her voice. "Has Lord Ponsby arrived?"

"Not yet." Caroline's eyes danced with excitement.

Other guests soon filled the doorway, and Susannah headed for the ballroom. Candlelight gleamed from fine beeswax candles in wall sconces and the chandelier. The hum of conversation was a welcome sound to Susannah, who now knew many of those present. She made her bows and stopped to chat where she could with one goal in mind. She had to find Winston.

She found him where she knew he would be—standing next to the large fireplace in the dining room. He looked devastatingly handsome in his evening dress, but he looked tired. She understood the strain he was under. Looking for proof against Caroline's father was taking its toll on both of them. But it went deeper with Winston, the dark smudges beneath his eyes confirmed it. The hard glint in his eye softened when his gaze connected with hers. She wondered what personal demons chased him so.

"Good evening," he said when she stood in front of him.

She watched him closely until he looked at the stickpin. He clearly recognized it. "Do you remember giving me this?" she finally asked when he said nothing.

"I remember."

"I wore it everyday until . . ." She stopped and looked away.

"Until when?" he whispered.

"Until I came to London," she finally said. "I was resigned to giving up your memory."

"I understand," he said, and she knew that he did. "Perhaps you should have thrown it away."

"I could not. It means too much to me."

"Susannah," he said, with remorse shining from his eyes. "Forgive me for all of this."

"I do, Winston. Truly, I do." She wanted to talk more but knew that they had precious little time to enter Lord Dunsford's rooms before dinner was announced. "Are we ready?"

Winston became her spy partner in an instant. "We should separate and then meet outside of Dunsford's room, under the portrait in ten minutes."

"Yes." Susannah felt the thrill of the search take over. Despite her distaste of the possible outcome, she had to own that the excitement of spying under stealth was undeniable. Every nerve ending in her body came alive.

"Check your timepiece," he said. "I have five minutes after the hour of nine o'clock."

Susannah pulled a small watch out of the pocket of her dress. "Yes, that is what I have as well."

"Very well. Dinner is not served for at least another hour. Until a quarter past."

Susannah agreed, then she walked away to join Lady Evelyn and the group of matrons surrounding her.

Winston watched her go. He did not feel much like making small talk with people he did not care about.

The last two weeks had been sheer torture for him. He had called upon Susannah often. The two of them had called upon Miss Dunsford with Lord Ponsby in tow, and he kept slamming into the desire to make time stand still. He enjoyed their foursome of friends far too much. It made his mission that much more difficult.

His feelings for Susannah had increased as well. She was incredibly levelheaded. He knew how much she wrestled with guilt, but she understood the importance of the security of the Crown. He had been the one who needed to remind himself of that duty. He did not wish to find any sort of letter; in fact, he was more than tempted to let the matter slide altogether. But he was honor bound to see this thing through to the end. His word as a gentleman was something he did not take lightly, nor cast aside when things got uncomfortable for him.

He checked his watch. Not yet time. He looked about at the young misses in white. The older, newly married ladies from last year's Season, dressed in jewel tones, stood on the arms of their husbands much like precious stones themselves. The *ton* was a world of consequence that he cared little about. But Susannah moved with ease within these circles, even if she physically moved with caution.

She was a dear, clumsy, sweetheart, and she had kept his pin. All these years she wore it every day. No wonder Lord Sheldrake had been angry with him. Susannah's heart had been breaking since he had left three years ago. He had callously let it continue, thinking she would have forgotten about him, thinking her too young to truly love him. He had been a fool. He could have written to her. He could have broken off the ties he had to her. She might have been married by now to a noble lad who deserved her. Instead, she had waited for him.

He suffered a sense of deep guilt as well as incredible relief. Somehow he could not imagine her with any other man but himself. Perhaps that was why he had never written to her. He had hoped with pure selfishness that she would wait for him. He did not want to love her and yet what choice did he have? Perhaps it was time for him to surrender his heart and be done with it.

He checked his watch again and meandered down the hall toward the kitchens. He ran quietly up the servants' stairs undetected. Silently he went until he reached a set of double doors at the far end of the second-floor hall next to a huge portrait. He checked his watch again—nine-twenty.

Susannah walked toward him. She tripped on something, but did not fall. "Quick," he whispered as he tried the double doors. They opened easily. "In here."

Susannah darted past him. He caught the scent of her cologne, and it teased him to get closer and sniff again. He shook his head. They did not have much time.

"Where should we start?" she asked, breathless.

"Let's start at this corner and each work our way in opposite directions until we meet." He pointed at the next set of double doors. "Go ahead. I am going to look behind those a moment." He glanced around the sitting room and realized that Lord Dunsford kept rather sparse furnishings even though they were of the finest quality.

He looked back at Susannah as she felt along the wall, checking behind paintings, running her hands along the moldings. She worked quickly yet she was thorough. He had taught her well.

He stepped through the second set of doors that opened easily under his touch, and he entered a bed-chamber. Something bothered him, but he could not quite place his finger upon it. Uneasiness caused the hairs on his neck to stand on end. He shook the feel-ing off. A dressing room appeared to the left, its door ajar. It would take too much time to search all of it. He would have to come back, somehow. He returned to the main sitting room. He worked opposite from Susannah, feeling every angle, looking behind each wall hanging. When they finally met, neither had found a secret hiding place. He rubbed the back of his neck. "Let us try the floor."

They were on their hands and knees, feeling the floorboards, when Winston sat back on his haunches. "This makes no sense," he muttered. "There should be a safe here somewhere. Most people keep them in their blasted studies or libraries." He still felt uneasy, and then he heard the noise.

"Someone is coming," Susannah hissed with fear-widened eyes.

Winston got up in an instant and grabbed her hand, pulling her with him to the heavy brocade curtains. They slipped behind them, and Winston was grateful that the material bunched on the floor and covered their feet. He heard the door open. He peeked through the slight crack where the curtains met. Su-sannah stood next to him, her hand still resting in his. He thought he felt her tremble and gave her hand an encouraging squeeze. She did not let go.

Lord Dunsford entered the room with something in his hand. And that is when the reason for Winston's odd feeling hit him. The doors had been unlocked. The deuce! They could have been easily caught. Dunsford must have been in the room before they came. That would explain why the doors opened freely.

Winston could not see clearly but the stack in Dunsford's hands looked very much like a pile of banknotes. He held his breath and forcibly calmed his racing heart. The safe was in Dunsford's bedchamber! He strained his ears to listen. The telltale clicking sounds of a safe being opened could be heard, and his heart soared.

He looked at Susannah, who smiled back at him. She had heard the sounds, too. He remained still, but her scent was tickling his nose again. He held her hand a bit tighter, letting his thumb caress the softness of her skin. Her shoulder rubbed against his arm, and it was all he could do to keep from pulling her into his arms.

He tried to concentrate on the crack in the curtains. He watched Lord Dunsford exit his bedchamber and lock the door. Then he walked through the outer sitting room, and Winston heard the clink of those doors being locked. Two layers of double doors locked! That was not a good sign. Lord Dunsford appeared to be hiding something.

"Is he gone?" Susannah whispered.

"Yes." He let out his breath that he had been holding.

They remained for another moment before Winston pulled back the curtains and stepped out. He still held Susannah's hand. He pulled his watch out of his waistcoat pocket and checked the time. It was nearly ten o'clock; dinner would soon be served. "Come, we had better get back."

"But what of the safe? Should we not check the bedchamber while we are here?"

"We cannot be missed. It will have to wait until another opportunity presents itself. We know where it is."

"But who knows when that may be," Susannah said with worry in her eyes.

He reached up and caressed her cheek. "Trust me. It will keep for now."

Susannah spread her napkin upon her lap. She tried not to stare at Winston. She wanted reassurance, but knew that he had none to give. She glanced down the long linen-covered table to where Lord Dunsford sat at the head. The man had something to hide, she was sure of it. Poor Caroline!

The meal progressed, but Susannah had lost her appetite. She picked at her food and kept her conversation to polite responses. After dessert had been served, one of the guests asked about the Dunsford Masquerade, and Susannah found her attention immediately piqued.

Lord Dunsford stood to address the table. "Ladies and gentlemen," Lord Dunsford started, "of course I will hold the Dunsford Masquerade, but rather than give the details myself, I will allow my daughter to explain."

Susannah felt an immediate response to the news. This was the opportunity they needed to search Lord Dunsford's bedchamber for the safe. She glanced at Winston. He nodded. Obviously, he thought the same thing.

"This year's masquerade will be different," Caroline said. "Instead of inviting scads of people the usual way, I ask for your help in making up the guest list." Caroline motioned for servants to step forth. Six footmen proceeded to hand each guest five embossed cards.

"These cards should be used to invite whomever you wish. The only stipulation is that your guests must produce one of your own calling cards the night of the ball to gain entry to Dunsford House. This will keep some level of order to the event, but it will also ensure complete mystery as to the identity of the guests until midnight, when we must unmask. Now, do not delay in completing and sending your invitations, since the ball will be held one week from today at eight o'clock. That information has been provided on the cards."

There was a swift round of applause. The plan was indeed a clever one. The masquerade guest list would be a complete mystery. Susannah found that she very much looked forward to it. She would have to discuss the event at length with Winston, since this would no doubt be the perfect diversion for them to sneak away to Lord Dunsford's bedchamber.

"Now," Caroline continued once the crowd became silent again, "the musicians are here, and the ballroom will be open for dancing. Gentlemen, a room off of the ballroom has been provided for cards and port should you wish to retire there."

Excited murmurs were heard as people rose from the table. Susannah remained seated. Winston approached her immediately and sat down next to her.

"The masquerade is our chance," he whispered.

"I thought so as well," she added.

"We shall have to discuss a plan of action. I wish to get in there and back out as quickly as possible. But I do not think we should discuss it here, or even at your home. We need time to prepare this fully, as I believe it may be our best chance. We want the ability to disappear without notice. When can we be alone?"

Susannah tried to keep a level head at the idea of

being alone with Winston where they could actually talk without having to rush through a search for fear of discovery. "Tomorrow evening, Sheldrake is taking us to Vauxhall Gardens for the opening night. Perhaps you might meet me there. We could take a stroll and discuss your plan."

"Excellent. That will work nicely."

She looked at him then. She could tell that his mind was working furiously. "We have a full week to plan, Winston. Perhaps you should simply enjoy the rest of this evening."

He looked at her and smiled slightly. "You are right, of course."

"Of course." She took a deep breath and asked, "Would you care to dance with me?" She stood and held out her hand before he could refuse her.

"You will force me to enjoy myself, is that the idea?" Then he smiled and warmth shone from his eyes. She could have embraced him at that moment and blurted out how much she loved him. But she held back. She could not make any mistakes with him this time. Instead, she wiggled her fingers at him. "Most certainly. Now, come with me."

Winston took her hand and wrapped it around the crook of his elbow. He intended to heed her words. He would enjoy himself in her company and forget about everything else. They walked in silence, but Winston felt the anticipation building between them. He wanted to feel her in his arms and knew she wanted the same.

Couples formed in a set for the quadrille and his disappointment knifed through him. He was hoping for a waltz. They joined the other dancers and faced one another. Susannah's eyes were shining bright blue pools. He cursed himself for not having the courage to whisk her away to India, whether she wanted to go or not. Surely he could make her happy there if he tried.

She was his, and he was hers. It had been so since the moment they had met three years ago. She had often been his last thought before sleep took him. But he had given up any ideas of being worthy of her soon after accepting his position with the Foreign Office. Now that she knew to a degree what he had been doing the last two years, he wondered· if perhaps he should throw caution to the wind and offer for her. He wanted no one else. He loved no other.

Love.

He realized with complete certainty that he loved Susannah. The past weeks spent with her had proved that she was a dear friend to him. Their friendship only served to deepen his attraction for her. Their hands met as they turned and bobbed to the music. Around they danced, connected only by their hands and gaze, but he felt as if she was part of him.

Too soon the dance ended. The musicians teased them with strains of a waltz, and Winston was not about to leave Susannah's side. "I believe this is our dance," he whispered. He placed his hand at her waist and whirled her farther out onto the floor.

"Yes," she said breathlessly.

He did not care that her sister or even Lord Sheldrake looked on. He had effectively announced his interest in Susannah to everyone there by dancing two dances in a row. If he danced a third, he'd border on the improper.

"What are you thinking?" she asked.

"How beautiful you are."

"Really?" Her eyes widened. "Careful, Captain. You give me considerable hope."

"You must realize that there are far better men than me."

"Not in my opinion."

He pulled her closer, inhaling her scent. "I do not deserve you," he whispered.

Her hand slipped from his shoulder to rest at the nape of his neck. Her fingers wreaked sweet havoc as she played with the ends of his hair. "Perhaps you do, but you merely refuse to accept it."

His gaze rested on her lips. He had briefly touched them before, but he had not been able to truly taste her, feel the textures of her mouth. It was all he could do to keep from lowering his head and kissing her thoroughly, right there in the ballroom floor.

The music hummed through his ears, and his blood pumped through his veins. He wanted the moment to last forever. But he knew it could not. Without warning images of past assignments, where he had waltzed with women in order to gain information about their husbands flickered through his mind, souring his pleasure. He pulled Susannah closer in a desperate attempt to shield him from his past and the guilt he carried because of it.

Susannah felt the warm pressure of his hand at her back. His thumb was making tiny circles that weakened her knees. She willingly pushed closer to him, partly to keep herself from collapsing upon the floor and partly because a thread of wanton desire pulled her there.

She swallowed hard as she looked at him. She had succeeded in capturing his attention, and it was only a matter of time before his heart was completely hers, yet she felt a sliver of fear. She had never felt such strong feelings before. Her insides were on fire, and she felt nearly sick with the heat. The power Winston had over her body was indeed strong.

She knew they were pushing propriety by waltzing so closely entwined. If she continued to draw closer to Winston, Sheldrake would no doubt have something to say about it. She wanted Winston to offer for her freely of his own accord. She did not wish him to be coerced by her brother-in-law for the sake of her reputation. Such thoughts effectively cooled her feverish desire, and she pulled back slightly.

At the question in Winston's eyes, she whispered, "If I come much closer, I fear I may trip you."

"And that would be a bad thing indeed to end up in a pile upon the floor. I might not wish to get up, and then where would we be?"

She felt her cheeks turn hot. The two of them were like dry tinder, and any spark could easily engulf them in flames. "We would certainly be in deep trouble."

But he smiled at her with a devilish look. "I can think of nowhere I would rather be right now, than in *deep trouble* with you."

Now she felt positively dizzy. "Winston, please." She had never experienced the flirtatious side of him. His teasing tone nearly melted her resolve to remain proper. And she had once thought him a terrible flirt when he tried to court Caroline! Perhaps, she was simply too jealous to appreciate his efforts.

"Very well, I shall try to behave. But you were the one who told me to enjoy myself this evening." He finished with a wink of his eye.

Susannah smiled. He was relaxed, and she was glad for it. Tomorrow she would see him at Vauxhall. There they could be private. They needed to settle more between them than their plan to search Lord Dunsford's bedchamber.

Chapter Twelve

Susannah twiddled her fork in her fingers and pushed the thinly sliced ham around on her plate. She sat with her family in one of the supper boxes at Vauxhall Gardens. She suffered from the fidgets while she waited for Winston.

Olivia suddenly placed her hand upon Susannah's arm. "Are you all right, dear? You seem miles away."

"I am fine." But that was not completely true. Susannah was nervous and anxious and hundreds of other feelings all jumbled into one enormously distracted state of mind.

"Is Winston meeting you here tonight?"

She looked at her sister with surprise. "How did you know?"

"It is not very hard to guess. The two of you have been nearly inseparable of late. Will there be an announcement soon?"

"I do not know." Susannah was completely unprepared to answer such a question. Winston had flirted with her. He wanted her, but he had not given her any indication of his intentions to offer for her. But then she had given him every reason to believe that she would not leave England.

"I wager that you must be close," Olivia said.

Susannah sat quietly while Olivia turned to Lady Evelyn. Lord Sheldrake and Aunt Agatha chattered on about the exorbitant fees charged for the sparse portions of food they had ordered. As she looked at them, her heart felt full. She loved them dearly and could not imagine a life without them. If she did travel to India with Winston, how long would it be until she saw her family again?

She pulled on Olivia's sleeve. "What if Winston does not offer for me?" she whispered.

Olivia turned in her chair to look directly into her eyes. "But he will once he is confident of a positive answer. It is the way with men. They cannot have an offer hanging out there unaccepted."

Susannah nodded. Olivia was most likely correct. She wished that Winston would stay in England; it would make things so much easier for her.

Their meal of ham, chicken, biscuits, and cheese-cakes was soon finished, and still Susannah waited. She gazed about the open pavilion, where they were one table of at least a hundred others. They were positioned near the walkways, and it was easy to get lost in watching the hoards of people passing by. Opening night at Vauxhall Gardens was not to be missed. The sun had set, and dusk was encroaching. Lamps were soon lit along the walkways and in the pavilions. A soft hum of excitement floated in the air as strains of music drifted on the cool evening breeze. Susannah continued to wait.

Finally, she saw him. Winston strolled toward her with a smile upon his face. He was taller than many men and the breadth of his shoulders drew admiring gazes from many ladies. Susannah's heart skipped a beat. He was clothed in full evening dress and he looked positively dashing.

"Good evening." He stood before their supper box.

"Why, Captain Jeffries, what a pleasant surprise," Lady Evelyn said.

Winston made his bows to each of them and added, "I hope you will forgive my interruption of your supper."

"Goodness, no, we have finished eating. Please join us," Olivia said.

"Thank you, but I wonder if I might escort Miss Lacey along the Grand Walk."

Susannah looked at Sheldrake for permission, knowing that of them all, he would be the one likely to deny Winston's request.

"You may. After the fireworks, do join us for sweetmeats and a pitcher of arrack punch," Sheldrake said. Olivia looked on with pride. Her sister had obviously coached Sheldrake in this matter, and Susannah would be forever grateful to her.

Susannah rose from her seat and impulsively gave Sheldrake a quick kiss upon the cheek. "Thank you," she whispered.

"Be careful," Sheldrake blurted, "there are devious young bucks about looking to make trouble."

"I shall keep Miss Lacey safe, my lord." Winston tucked her hand into the crook of his arm, his expression serious. The men had exchanged an underlying message that meant much more than simply protecting her from brigands.

"You look very fine this evening," he said when they were out of earshot of her family.

"Thank you. You do as well." Susannah remembered how long she had been waiting. "In fact, where have you been? I have waited this age for you to arrive."

"Dinner party," he explained. "I had to meet with Lord Castlereagh to advise him of our progress."

Susannah turned to look at him in surprise. "He knows that I am helping you? What did he say?"

"He was not pleased, but understood once I told him the details of the situation. He will attend the Dunsford Masquerade as well. If we find that letter, I shall deliver it directly to Castlereagh."

Susannah sighed. "I see." She looked down at her slippers to hide the disgust she felt at her part in Lord Dunsford's ruination. It was her duty to help Winston uncover a traitor if Lord Dunsford was in fact that.

He patted her hand. "Soon, it will be over, and we can put this behind us."

"But it will be the very beginning for Caroline," Susannah whispered.

Winston did not say a word in response. He did not have to. They both knew the heartache that faced Caroline if her father committed treason. If they found a letter, they would effectively destroy Caroline's chances with Lord Ponsby. He looked up at the sky, then said, "Come, and let us find somewhere to sit down."

Susannah's emotions were in a jumble. "Winston," she asked when they were seated upon a bench near a small grove of trees. "Why must you choose India? Can you not ask for an arrangement here in England?" She felt his arm tense beneath her hand, and knew that his answer was not what she wished to hear.

"I go to India for two reasons. The first is that Castlereagh has promised to give me a post with the military there if I complete this assignment successfully.

He has excellent connections, and it will allow me to quit the secret service for good."

When he hesitated, she urged him on, "And the second?"

"The second and most important reason is that I have given Ponsby my word."

"Lord Ponsby?"

"I have become his partner in a spice business that he has purchased. Ponsby needs someone on-site to oversee the operation. It promises to be an excellent opportunity."

"I see." Susannah bit her lower lip. "You will finally find your fortune in India."

"Precisely," he said.

"How long must you reside there?" Perhaps she could wait for him.

"Until the business venture turns a profit." He took both of her hands into his own. "Susannah, it could take years."

"When did you enter into this partnership with Lord Ponsby?" She wondered if he had entered this agreement to escape from her.

"Soon after I arrived in England. The papers were drawn, and I have signed them. It is quite official."

Susannah remained silent. His decision had been sealed before they had forged any kind of attachment. She tried not to blame him, but it was difficult.

"Forgive me," he whispered.

"Whatever for? Your decision was made before we—" She stopped. Her throat had gone dry. He could no doubt see the struggle going on inside of her. He was not going to offer for her. Susannah realized that even if he did, she was not sure she could accept if it meant years away from everything she knew and loved. She knew he was headed for India, but she never believed it was permanent, until now. Her family or Winston, how could she possibly choose between them?

He pulled her into his arms. "I would never ask you to wait for me yet again. Perhaps it is best that we go our separate ways."

She felt hot tears stinging the corners of her eyes. She sniffed angrily. Sobbing would only make matters worse. She pushed out of his arms and sniffed again. "Winston," she said, avoiding a scene, "we must make our plans for the masquerade."

"Agreed." Winston felt lower than dirt. Accepting Ponsby's business offer was the right thing to do. He had not realized then what he would feel now. There was no going back. He gave his word. His word as a gentleman was all he had.

He only hoped that Susannah might consider going with him, but he could not ask it of her. He could not ask her to choose between him and her family. Perhaps it was better this way, he thought. His gut wrenched at the thought that after all this time apart from one another, they had come together only to be split apart again. Destiny played a cruel joke upon them both. He watched her as she bravely replaced her sorrow with a false cheeriness that he found more disturbing than if she had burst into tears. Winston agreed, "Yes, we need to plan."

Susannah stood next to Winston with her head tilted toward the sky that erupted in a blaze of light and color. The firework display was prodigiously fine. She had never seen such a sight, and despite her heavy heart, she applauded vigorously. She was acutely aware of a somber Winston, who stood next to her.

They had made a plan. At the Dunsford Masquerade, they would meet in the upstairs hallway below the portrait at half past nine o'clock. It would give them little more than two solid hours of searching Lord Dunsford's bedchamber before they must return to the party and unmask at midnight. No one should miss them, since they agreed to tell no one their costumes.

The popping of fireworks and the appreciative murmurs of the spectators rang in her ears, but the sensation gave her an isolated feeling, as if she were alone amid the crowd. She glanced at Winston, and he smiled but it did not reach his eyes, and she felt her heart twist anew. He was honor bound to go to India. She would not dream of asking him to break his word. Winston valued honor deeply; it was one of the many things she admired in him. Olivia had been right. Winston would not offer marriage if he believed he might not be accepted. If Susannah wished to marry Winston, it was up to her to let him know her answer before the question was ever asked.

She fiddled with the string of her reticule. Was it better to regret her choice to leave her family or let Winston go? She could not possibly expect him to wait for her decision. It might take years before his work in India was done.

The fireworks ended and Winston took her hand in his. "We had best return to your supper box."

"Yes," Susannah whispered. She tried to appear normal, not steeped in thought.

They walked back in silence along the Grand Walk, dodging and weaving through the thick crowd. Winston held onto her hand, and she clung to him as if he was leaving her tomorrow. When they approached the supper box, a servant delivered a pitcher of Vauxhall's famous punch.

"Splendid," Sheldrake said loudly. "Your timing is perfect."

"Perfect indeed." Winston pulled out a chair for her.

Sheldrake did the honors of pouring the liquor into each glass. Susannah brought the punch to her nose and sniffed. It smelled strong and she wrinkled her nose.

"Go ahead," Winston encouraged her. "Taste it. It is quite good."

Susannah noted the disappointment in Winston's eye, when she hesitated. She suddenly realized that although she cherished stories of great daring, such as those by Mrs. Radcliff, she was far too timid to taste new foods. She surrounded herself with that which was comfortable and familiar. Perhaps it was time she took a risk.

She brought the glass to her lips and let the sweet liquor linger there before she tipped the glass and emptied the contents with one gulp. She blinked as the punch burned a sugary sweet path down her throat.

Winston laughed. "Sip it, Susannah. You have to sip it."

Sheldrake chimed in, "It'll go straight to her head now."

Olivia giggled, as did Lady Evelyn.

"Oh, pish," Aunt Agatha scoffed. "Give her another glass so she can taste it."

Winston reached out to refill her glass. When he stopped at less than an inch of liquid, she tipped his hand to pour more.

"Careful now," he murmured. "Sip it slowly."

Warmth had spread through her body. She was determined to stretch herself into taking risks. The sweetmeats arrived and the platter was passed around.

Susannah chose something completely new. She bit into a soft confection of coconut and honey. It was delicious.

Susannah felt a swell of contentment bubble within her as she looked around the table at her dearly loved family. Aunt Agatha hooted at the jugglers who stopped to perform in front of their table. Lady Evelyn's eyes were falling closed, and her head bobbed down toward her chest. Sheldrake and Olivia made sheep's eyes at one another.

It dawned on her that she did not have to choose between Winston and her family. She would always have her family's love no matter how far away she traveled. She glanced at Winston, and her heart swelled with pride. He was different than the man she had fallen in love with three years ago, but she loved him more now than she had ever thought possible. Perhaps it was time she considered moving to India.

Susannah rushed up the stairs of Dunsford House and down the hall to Caroline's rooms. "I came as fast as I could," Susannah said as she entered. "Caroline, what is it? Your note said to come straightaway."

"I need your help." Caroline paced back and forth.

A tremor of fear raced up Susannah's spine. "You have it."

"You will think me silly, but I need your advice. Short of seducing the man, I do not know how to make it clear to Lord Ponsby that I wish to wed him. He treats me with such a polite regard that I fear I shall scream the next time I am with him. I have seen the longing in his eyes, but he acts as if he does not know my feelings."

Susannah let out a sigh of relief and sat upon the

bed. "My sister told me that a man would not offer for a lady unless he is quite certain of being accepted. Lord Ponsby might not know how serious your feelings are engaged."

"Then he is a fool," Caroline huffed.

"What you need to do is to send him a clear message."

"That is what I thought I have been doing."

Susannah had an idea. "Do you know what costume Lord Ponsby plans to wear?"

"No, I do not. Why?" Caroline asked.

"Well, we must find out, and you shall have to match him somehow. For instance, if he comes as Marc Antony, you must be his Cleopatra."

"That is the very thing and completely perfect!" Caroline sat upon the bed. "But what if he dresses in something staid and commonplace?"

Susannah slid off the bed to stand in front of her friend. "Then you must match his style completely."

"I would much rather be Cleopatra to his Marc Antony. Could you ask Winston to convince Lord Ponsby to dress as Marc Antony?"

Susannah giggled. It was certainly worth a try. Besides, it would give her an excuse to see Winston again. "Of course, I shall ask him."

Caroline stood up and gave her a quick hug. "Wonderful. Now, what do you plan to wear as your costume?"

"I do not know." Susannah could not tell Caroline what she planned to wear, even though she was not entirely sure. Guilt ripped through her. She did not like keeping secrets from her friend.

"Oh! Susannah, I am such a pea-goose," Caroline said.

"Why, dear?"

"Come with me to the attics. There are clothes stored there that my father brought back from his travels. There are gowns from India and Egypt that my mother wore. I am quite certain that we shall find the perfect gown for Cleopatra. And we might find something for you, too."

Susannah followed and her mind raced. She would heed her own advice. She would send Winston the message of her desire to go with him by the costume she chose. It was indeed a perfect plan!

The night of the Dunsford Masquerade arrived, and it had established itself as the event of the Season. The *ton* was abuzz with titters and gossip regarding who might be present and what they might wear.

Susannah sat at her vanity while Botts made a sleek cap of her hair with clove-scented pomade. Tonight both she and Caroline planned to capture their men once and for all. She smiled when she thought of how splendid Caroline would look as Cleopatra. They had found several suitable gowns in the attics of Dunsford House, and Susannah had borrowed two as well as a gorgeous length of Indian silk. Her heart raced when she thought of what Winston's reaction might be when he saw her choice of costume.

She had to own that she was as nervous as she was excited. Anxiety filled her. Tonight they might find the letter they had been searching for, and she tried to prepare herself for consequences that might follow.

She had seen Winston only twice in the last week. They had spoken little about their futures or their feelings, and focused on revisiting their plan of action in searching Lord Dunsford's bedchamber. Despite feelings of unrequited love, their friendship remained true.

It had been hard not to tell Winston that she wanted to go to India with him, but purposefully she held back. She needed to be absolutely sure before she gave Winston the sign he needed in order to offer for her.

A heady anticipation filled her. Her jitters and fidgets were worse than the day she had been presented at court. As Botts helped her into her costume, she felt a surge of panic. Was she making the right decision? Would she be happy in India, far away from her family?

A light knock at the door brought Susannah's head up. "Come in," she said.

"Goodness, Susannah. You look breathtaking," Olivia said as she entered the room. Olivia dressed as Juliet in emerald velvet—Sheldrake was her Romeo.

"Thank you." Susannah hesitated then finally said, "Might we speak a moment?"

"Of course. What is it?" Her sister motioned for her to come sit by the fire.

"Botts, if you would, please see if my black pelisse has been pressed." Susannah needed to be private with her sister. She waited until her maid had left before she sat down next to her sister.

"Tell me what troubles you," Olivia said.

Susannah let out a deep breath. "I have not told you, but Winston has entered into a partnership with Lord Ponsby that will take him to India for several years. It is a splendid opportunity and . . ." She stopped and looked down at her fingers. A lump had formed in her throat, and she felt terribly close to tears. She did not expect it to be so difficult to explain her intentions to her family.

Her sister reached out and squeezed her hand. "I know, dear. I know all about it."

Susannah looked up quickly. "How?"

"Richard has told me. Your Winston explained his prospects to him weeks ago, when he dined with us. I understand completely if you decide to go with him. I do not believe it wise for you both to wait yet again. And I promise that when George is a little older, we shall come and visit you there."

Tears tripped over Susannah's lids and ran down her face. She was speechless. Her dearest sister and most loved of all people, had just given her what she found that she needed to move forward. Olivia had given her approval. "Thank you," she croaked.

Olivia embraced her.

Susannah squeezed her sister with all her might. "I shall miss you all so," she whispered.

"I know." Olivia's voice was trembling, too. "But you must follow your heart. Winston is a good man. Richard and I both know that he will make you happy."

Susannah pulled back from her sister with a sense of relief and much needed peace. What she was about to do was right. She would make sure Winston understood that it was her choice and deepest desire to go with him to India and be his wife.

Chapter Thirteen

*W*inston entered Dunsford House's ballroom. He was glad that he had decided upon his cavalry uniform. There were several gentlemen dressed in various military uniforms and some dressed in dragoon colors of red coats and white breeches. Even though the black facings and silver laces distinguished him as a Second Queen's Dragoon Guard, still his choice had been perfect. He would attract little attention, and his absence would go unnoticed. The black mask he wore did not completely hide his identity, but then Susannah was likely the only person who would truly look for him.

Helping himself to the champagne punch that was offered, he looked about the ballroom that was filled with a sea of costumes. He saw kings and queens and fabled heroes scattered everywhere. Laughter filled the air. Masquerades brought out not only merriment, but also a devilish cord of mischief in the guests.

He noticed Ponsby, standing in a Roman-styled white tunic near the fireplace, and he chuckled. Poor Ponsby's costume would not do well on this unseasonably chilly night. He sipped his punch and looked for Susannah. The last time they had spoken, she was still undecided upon her costume. He pictured her dressed as an angel complete with halo and wings.

She had been his avenging angel last night. His dream had taken an odd turn from the usual nightmare. In his dream, Susannah had stepped in front of him after he had killed one of many enemy soldiers. Instead of recoiling in horror at what he had done, she had simply taken his hand and pulled him away from the carnage of bodies laying about his feet into a grassy meadow where birds sang and the sun shined brilliantly. When he woke after nearly a full night's sleep he felt oddly at peace. It was a most welcome respite from his constant tossing and turning.

He checked his watch. It was nine o'clock and still he had not seen Susannah. But then, there were no ladies dressed as angels. He spent the next half hour mingling and making conversation where he could. It was interesting to converse with someone completely in disguise. Some individuals he identified, but many remained a mystery. The more he wandered through the crowd, the more anxious and nervous he became. Tonight he needed to find that safe.

After chatting endlessly with a guest he knew he'd not remember, he checked his watch again and finally it was time to meet Susannah. He bounded up the main stairs, anticipation pounding in his veins. He wanted this business with Dunsford over. He stopped upon the landing when he spotted the woman waiting below the huge portrait.

It could only be Susannah, but she looked too exotic, too forbidden. His heart raced. She was dressed as an Indian princess complete with headpiece and veil that revealed only her eyes, which now gazed into his own. The printed silk draped her slender figure to perfection. Her hair had been slicked back, and the headpiece of jewels rested low upon her forehead, a huge ruby dangling between her bright blue eyes.

"Susannah," he breathed. If her costume was any indication of her intentions, he was not going to leave England alone.

She walked toward him, a look of indecent determination in her eyes. "I hope you understand the meaning of my costume. I do not know exactly what they wear in India, but I would like to find out firsthand if you wish to take me there."

"I did not dare to hope," he said as he brought her hands to his lips to kiss each ringed finger.

"I will not let life pass by for the sake of staying in England. My happiness can no longer afford to play it safe," she said firmly. "I must go where you go. You will be my home."

His heart was so full he feared that he would blurt an offer of marriage right there, but he could not, not yet. He had Sheldrake to approach and this business with Dunsford to finish before he could ask for her hand. He knew she would accept him, and that made his mind near dizzy with joy.

"Thank you," he whispered, knowing he was not nearly conveying the depth of his feelings. "Come, we had best break in." He tried to focus his energy on that task at hand, but he kept thinking of their future together. His dream might have been an omen, and that gave him courage. He had yet to tell Susannah the reasons for his nightmares, but he knew that when the time was right, he would tell her all of it. He only hoped that she would not feel differently toward him.

Susannah watched Winston pick the lock to Lord Dunsford's apartments. The hallway remained quiet. She heard nothing but the ticks of Winston's work.

Her heart pounded in tandem with the clicks that echoed through the hallway.

He looked up at her with a smile and a wink when he opened the door. He looked incredible in uniform, and the mask he had donned gave him an air of dangerous allure that she found unsettling to her breathing.

"Entre' vous, mademoiselle," he whispered as he pushed the door open.

"You are quite talented," she whispered back.

"One has to be creative when one is a spy."

"I can imagine," she answered with a broad smile. Her costume had worked! An offer was imminent.

Lord Ponsby felt a little ridiculous and more than a bit under dressed in his Roman tunic and leather jerkin. His hair was newly cut à la Brutus, which he had to own, made him look like the famous general Marc Antony. He wore a small mask across his eyes and carried a sword. Winston reminded him to keep Caroline busy, which would be as easy as it was pleasurable.

But he had to find her. He had come to the conclusion that he must offer for her regardless of what her father might have done. He loved her. The last two weeks spent calling upon her had been sheer bliss. She was perfect in every way except for the suspicions surrounding her father.

It had taken these last two weeks for him to realize that he could not leave Caroline alone to face her father's treason if such a thing was proven. She would need him, and he was not about to let her down. His plan was to marry her quickly before any news of her father's dealings could be known. If she'd have him.

A tap upon his shoulder brought him around, and his breath caught in his throat.

"My lover, Marc Antony, has finally come," Caroline said in a sultry voice.

"Caro, my word, you look smashing." He ogled her shamelessly.

She giggled and twirled about for his inspection.

He let his gaze travel over every tantalizing inch of her. She dressed in a simple white gown that had no sleeves and a plunging neckline. She wore gold bracelets on her arms and gold around her neck and in her dark hair. She was his Cleopatra, and he was hardpressed not to pull her into his arms right there and then.

Caroline smiled when she saw the heated appreciation in his gaze. It was not fair truly, since she had already taken her fill of looking at him before she crept up behind him. His strong legs were bare from the knees down to the tops of his leather sandals.

He took hold of her hand and pulled her aside. "Where can we go to be private?"

Her heart beat wildly. And she had planned to seduce him this evening! He appeared to have the same goal in mind. She had to own that she was shocked, and a little nervous. Lord Ponsby, the most frustratingly polite and honorably behaved suitor she had ever known, was looking at her now as if he wanted to throw her over his shoulder and whisk her up the stairs. In the costume he wore, he looked like a warrior of old who would not hesitate to act upon such desires.

"What is it that you have in mind?" She tried to sound seductive, but her voice came out a mere squeak.

He stepped closer and with his arm about her waist, he pulled her to him.

She found herself crushed against the jerkin he

wore, and the scent of leather mixed with his cologne was a heady scent that made her knees weak. She leaned against him. "Lord Ponsby," she whispered, "we are in the hall."

"William," he said.

"What?"

"My given name is William. You must know my Christian name if we are to be wed."

She melted against him, dizzy with happiness. "What did you say?"

"You, my bold little Cleopatra, are not bold at all. Since you refuse to take me somewhere private, I shall ask you here and now. Be my wife, Caroline, and make me the happiest of men."

She threw her arms about him and placed her lips upon his for the completion of the kiss they once started. It took only a moment for William to deepen it instantly.

When they finally broke apart, he asked, "Does that mean yes?"

"Yes, oh, yes," she breathed before she kissed him again.

Susannah and Winston searched Lord Dunsford's bedchamber for nearly half an hour, and still they had not found the safe.

"This doesn't make sense," Winston said as he stood in the center of the room looking bewildered. "We have gone over this room with a fine comb, and still we cannot find that safe. I know it is here. It must be."

Susannah shifted from one foot to the other. Her head ached from the tension that had been building in her ever since they had entered Lord Dunsford's rooms. She rubbed her neck, but found little relief.

She was as anxious as Winston to be done with this mission.

She let her gaze wander over the room. Slowly, she studied each corner, each painting, but had no new ideas where they should look next. "Perhaps we should check the fireplace again."

Winston shrugged his shoulders and agreed.

They stood at either end of the large stone mantel and felt along the edge and underneath and along the sides, fingering each stone and each crevice. Nothing!

And then they heard the sound of a key jiggling in the door.

"Quick." Winston grabbed hold of her arm. "Under the bed."

Susannah did not protest. She moved as fast as she was able. Her heart pounded in her ears, and her breath came in short gasps as she slid under the large four-poster bed. Winston dove under behind her and wrapped his arm protectively over her. She tried to calm herself, but instead she trembled. She clamped a hand over her mouth to make sure she did not utter a sound.

She lay there watching with wide eyes while Winston peeked out under the bed linen that he gently lifted with his ornamental saber. Had he pulled it out of his scabbard intent on using it if he had to? The thought made her shiver. "Do you see anything?" she said in the faintest of whispers.

He shook his head. "No," he breathed.

They listened to the footsteps coming toward them. Both of them lay on their bellies, peering out of the tiny lift of the bed's linens. She wiggled closer against Winston. The strength of him gave her courage, and her trembles subsided.

She strained her ears in an attempt to hear what

the man was doing. It had to be Lord Dunsford who whistled mere feet from them.

"Of course," Winston whispered after Dunsford walked away from the bed to clang about in his dressing room.

"What?"

"We never searched his dressing room," he whispered. "How stupid of me."

Susannah wanted to tell him that he had much on his mind, when the footsteps returned to the bedchamber. She saw two feet right in front of the bed and she held her breath.

Winston let the bed linen drop as he carefully pulled back the saber, and lay completely still, his face turned toward hers.

She stared at him. If they were caught, it would be more than a scandal. It would be construed as a crime. Winston had once told her that the Foreign Office pleaded ignorance when a special information officer was caught. No wonder he wanted a simple post in India, she thought.

She reached over and brushed the stray hair that had fallen across his forehead. He had long since taken off his mask, and she gazed at his face with love swelling in her heart. The dark smudges beneath his eyes were not so pronounced this evening.

He smiled at her with desire in his eyes, and she felt herself flush. The threat of discovery added urgency to the sensations running through her. She felt quite daring as she let her fingers caress his face. Every part of her hummed with awareness of how close they were. She let her fingers trail down his cheek to his lips, and he kissed them.

It was not enough. He lifted her veil. A tremor ran through her when she realized that he was going to kiss her. Her body felt like it would melt under his heated gaze. Closer his face came to hers, closing the already short distance between them.

She could no longer keep her eyes open, and when Winston's lips connected with her own, she sighed deeply. He held the back of her head, his fingers threading through her slicked-back hair, wreaking havoc with the jeweled headpiece. She did not care. She clung to his lips.

Winston forgot about Lord Dunsford walking just inches away from the bed. He forgot about his mission, his plans for India, his fear of Susannah's rejection and his past deeds. He was completely lost the instant Susannah parted her lips. All that mattered to him was this, their first real kiss. Her sweet innocence cautioned him to tread carefully, yet his desire raged like a bonfire. It was quick and hot and blazing toward the sky.

He heard her soft moan and knew they were in danger of being discovered if they carried on any further. He tried to pull away, but she would have none of it. With sweet abandon, she grabbed hold of his face with both of her hands and nearly smothered him with kisses.

"Winston, I have wished for you to kiss me this age," she whispered.

"Sshhhhh," he said. He feared for the volume of her voice, and he had no idea whether or not Dunsford was still in the room.

"But I . . ."

There was only one way to silence her. He kissed her again. She parted her lips and tangled her tongue about his. He was the one who moaned.

"Susannah," he panted when they broke apart.

"Dunsford." He cocked his head and nodded toward the dressing room.

She flushed a deep red to the roots of her now chaotic hair and nodded. He loved her. He swore a silent oath that he would do his best to make her never regret leaving England.

After listening intently for what seemed like an eternity, Winston concluded that Dunsford had gone. He flipped up the bed linen with his saber again, and peered out into a still and quiet room. No one moved. Dunsford must have left while they had kissed. "I think it is clear," he whispered as he slid out from underneath the bed.

She scuffled out behind him, and he bent to help her. Her costume had not suffered too much for their adventure, but her headpiece was crooked and her hair stuck out in different directions. Her lips were delectably swollen. He was tempted beyond reason to taste them yet again. His gaze wandered to the bed. He shook his head to clear his wayward thoughts. "We had best check the dressing room," he said. "There should be a mirror where you can tidy yourself."

She smoothed back her hair, but still looked slightly dazed. They had already lost much time. He took her hand and pulled her along into the dressing room. It was filled with armoires and shelves and a copper tub for bathing. Winston did not bother to do a thorough search. He focused immediately on the only painting upon the wall. Perhaps, the safe was behind it.

He looked back to see Susannah adjusting her costume in the cheval mirror. Drawn by the sight of her, he watched her run her finger over her lips. She looked up and their gaze connected in the glass and he could not look away.

"Winston, the safe," she reminded him.

He nodded. They had so much to discuss and plan for their lives, but it must wait. He felt along the edges of the painting and pulled it down. The safe lay behind it, built into the wall. He easily compromised the lock and gained entry. The compartment was filled with banknotes, gold coins, and various jewels. A stack of papers caught his eye. If it existed, the letter would be within this stack. Carefully, he pulled out the bundle of documents. He sat down upon a chair, ready to thoroughly examine each piece of parchment. "Check the hallway, will you?" he asked Susannah.

"Certainly." She frowned deeply as she eyed the bundle of papers. Despite the pain it would cause to those he cared about, he almost wished for the letter to be there. He wanted nothing more than the military post with an income to support Susannah. As he shuffled the papers, seeking proof of treason, his hands shook—so much was at stake.

He looked closely at the papers. The majority of them were IOUs with Dunsford the one to collect. This was the reason he continually came into his bedchamber during parties. This was the reason for the locked rooms. Lord Dunsford was a gambler.

Winston scratched his head. There was no letter from Napoleon. There were only IOUs. Dunsford had amassed a considerable amount of wealth by winning at cards against very prominent men. And yet he still had the gall to travel as a diplomat in the name of England, all the while fleecing her betters!

He heard Susannah's gasp and then voices. Someone had come. Panic filled him as he hurried to straighten the stack into their original order.

"Jeffries," a man's voice called out. The deuce! It was Castlereagh.

"He asked to see you," Susannah explained as she led the Secretary of Foreign Affairs into Lord Dunsford's dressing room. Castlereagh was dressed in complete evening attire save for the mask he wore. Completely unoriginal, but expected, Winston thought. The man had little imagination.

"Thank God," Castlereagh muttered. "Quickly put everything back the way you found it."

"I am endeavoring to do so, my lord." Winston did not like the implications of Castlereagh's flustered demeanor. Something was wrong.

He looked up at Susannah, who stood in the doorway of the dressing room wringing her hands. He braced himself for the worst. "What is it?" he asked.

"There has been a grave mistake. Dunsford has never had dealings with Napoleon or his supporters."

"But the list you received." Winston felt the air leave his lungs.

"Falsified. I have just recently met with the Prince Regent. Dunsford is a favorite of his. When he found out that we were investigating him, well let us simply say it did not go over well."

"I see." Winston managed to choke out.

"So there is no letter?" Susannah asked eagerly.

"No, not for Dunsford at least. I have another officer looking into the source of our *list*," Castlereagh said.

Winston did not know what to feel. All this time and energy had been wasted, his money spent. "My lord, about my requested post," he blurted.

"Sorry, dear boy," Castlereagh said. "I spoke too soon. The resources are diminished, and there are others in front of you I am afraid. You are finally free to do as you will. Your excellent service is no longer needed. Come by tomorrow and I will settle your expenses."

"Yes, my lord," Winston said with a lifeless voice. He had just been given a severe blow. He needed that blasted post for an income!

"Do hurry and exit Dunsford's apartments." Lord Castlereagh took his leave.

"Yes, of course," Winston whispered. He sat completely still for a moment, then went about the business of putting everything back to rights. He was trying very hard not to look at Susannah.

"Oh, Winston," she said with a peal of genuine glee. "Is that not splendid? Now Lord Ponsby can freely marry Caroline, and she needn't be ruined. I am so very happy."

He placed the documents in the safe and closed it. He stepped away only to be nearly knocked off his feet as Susannah launched herself into his arms.

"Winston, are you not pleased! We can go to India and be married without having to worry about Caroline."

He wrapped his arms about her and squeezed her tight, unable to trust his voice at the moment. How could he possibly marry her when he had no income to support her?

Chapter Fourteen

Susannah knew something was wrong. She wanted to savor the relief she felt but instead she worried. Surely it was nothing more than Winston's disappointment in not getting his requested post, she told herself.

Shrugging off feelings of dread, she quickly made her way down the main staircase while Winston used the servants' stairs. The clock on the wall read half past eleven o'clock. Susannah rushed into the ballroom looking about for Winston. When she saw Caroline instead, Susannah ran to her.

"Susannah." Caroline set down her cup of punch and dashed toward her. "My goodness, where have you been? I have not seen you since you first arrived."

They met halfway and clasped hands. "I have been . . ." Susannah started only to be interrupted by her ecstatic friend.

"I have the most wonderful news," Caroline gushed. "Ponsby has asked me to marry him!"

"Oh, that is famous!"

"Yes," Caroline breathed. "Ponsby is telling Winston this very moment. The two are in business together, did you know?"

"Yes, Winston has told me. It will take him to India, and that is why I dressed as an Indian Princess. I plan to go with him if he will offer for me. I shall simply die without him, I think."

Caroline, still holding her hands, gave her a quick squeeze. "I know exactly how you feel."

"Dunsford is free of all suspicion?" Ponsby asked.

"Yes, completely cleared." Winston clasped his hands firmly behind his back.

"Good show!" Ponsby slapped him on the back. "I have asked Caro to be my wife. I planned on dealing with the treason when the time came, which I hoped would be after the wedding. I cannot tell you how relieved this makes me feel."

"I understand," Winston said quietly. "Congratulations, my friend." He reached out to shake Ponsby's hand. "You deserve this happiness."

"So then what is it that bothers you?" Ponsby had come to know him well.

"I have lost the post. Castlereagh has given it to another," he said with a dull voice.

"Egad, I am sorry, old boy." Winston knew that in his state of exuberance, Ponsby did not fully understand what this loss meant.

Winston considered his options. He could not offer for Susannah with no means of support. It wasn't to be borne. He had failed to provide for her, and because of that they would have to wait. And that would be sheer agony for them both. Perhaps the best thing to do was end it here and now.

The clock struck midnight, and then it chimed twelve times. A hush had settled over the crowd in anticipation of unmasking as everyone stood in the ballroom waiting. The flicker of candlelight seemed to still as if it, too, wished to know the identities of those present. The time had come. Susannah watched with bemused delight as Caroline stood on the musician's platform to announce that all guests must remove their masks on the count of three.

"One," the crowd shouted.

A tremor of excitement raced along Susannah's spine, partly because the exuberance Caroline demonstrated as she counted down was infectious. It was near impossible not to get caught up in this moment of disclosure.

"Two!"

"We need to talk."

"Three!"

Susannah turned to find Winston at her elbow. Ladies and gentlemen unmasked all around them with laughter. She let the veil drop away from her face but she felt her smile die at the expression he wore. There was no trace of merriment in his eyes. "What is the matter?"

"May we speak privately?"

Her heart skipped a beat. Was he planning to offer for her? But if that were so, surely he would look happy. The uneasy feeling returned with full force. "Of course."

The musicians played a fast-paced country-dance that closely matched the boisterous crowd. She longed to pull Winston into a set, but first things first. The matter of their engagement needed to be dealt with between them so that they could approach Sheldrake on the morrow.

She followed Winston's back as he wove a path for them through the throngs of guests until they reached a bench that had been turned into a secretive alcove by latticework trellises covered in greenery. A perfect place for a proposal, she thought with a smile.

Winston waited while she sat down, but instead of

sitting next to her or even bending down on one knee, he paced.

"Winston, what is it? Have you not asked me here to propose?" she said.

That stopped him, and he turned anguished eyes upon her. "More than anything, Susannah, I wish that I could." He mopped his brow and started pacing again.

Dread churned into real fear, and she shivered with it. "Then, why do you not?"

"Because I cannot, not without that post." He stood still before her.

She stood up as well. "Why?"

"I have no income, Susannah, none."

"But your partnership with Lord Ponsby . . ."

He cut her off. "Is not profitable nor will it turn a profit for some time. It could take years. I cannot support you. I cannot marry you."

She digested this information as if she had swallowed a ball of lead that hit her stomach with a painful thud. "I have a dowry," she said in a small voice.

He stood straighter, looking completely offended. "I will not marry you, Susannah, if I cannot provide for you. Nor will I ask that you wait for me yet again. It simply will not work for us. I am sorry."

Tears seared her lids until they leaked out and ran down her cheeks. She could not believe her ears. After all they had been through together, after their kisses just moments ago, it had come to this pass. He would not have her.

She bolted from him with a sob and dashed through the dining room into the hallway, pushing people aside as she went. No one noticed her distress, and she was glad for it. She closed the doors of the front parlor and threw herself upon the couch and cried. The stress of weeks of searching, of wanting Winston's love and finally coming close to having it only to be denied because of his cursed pride was more than she could bear. She sobbed until she was spent.

Winston let her go. There was nothing more he could do. It hurt like the very devil, but he knew it was for the best. He would not take her to the ends of the earth away from her family and the luxuries she had grown accustomed to only to watch her love turn into resentment when he could not support them. He'd not live off her dowry, either. That money was hers to be spent as she saw fit as mistress of her own home.

He did not wish to remain at the masquerade nor did he wish to run into Lord Sheldrake, just now. He would explain the situation to Sheldrake when he felt more in control of himself, after he had a chance to get over the bleak emptiness that took hold of his soul.

Susannah sat before a blazing fire in her bedchamber with Winston's calling card in her hands. She had picked it up off the floor when they left the Dunsford Masquerade. After a good spell of weeping, a calming anger took over that gave her the strength to not only wipe her tears away, but to formulate a plan of action.

After seeking Caroline's maid to right her appearance, Susannah reentered the ballroom with a false smile upon her face. She pretended to enjoy herself immensely as she conversed with various acquaintances. She danced every dance. Winston, she noticed, stayed long enough to watch her waltz with some lord before he left. She decided that she would let him stew over his decision for now until she could confront him privately and speak her mind.

Fortunately, Lord Sheldrake and Olivia had not

known anything was amiss as they drove home. Susannah chatted gaily about the night's events and Caroline's plans to marry Lord Ponsby. As *she* would marry Winston. She would make him see reason, but not tonight. She doubted he would listen to her argument tonight.

She twiddled Winston's card between her fingers and knew what she must do. Caroline had said it once, and Susannah realized the sheer beauty of it. She would seduce Winston if she had to. Tomorrow morning, near dawn, she would sneak away to his residence and prove to him that he should not live without her.

Winston woke to hammering on the door. "Go away!" He yelled, but what came out was a muffled whisper. His head ached. He had tossed and turned what little of the night had remained after he arrived home.

The door opened, but he did not bother to look up. It must be Pegston to pick up the mess he had left when he returned in the wee hours after nursing a bottle of spirits at White's. He had tumbled over a couple of chairs and had broken a few things, too.

"My goodness, your room is a pigsty," a very feminine voice said.

His eyes opened. He peeked out from under his pillow, and there she was, like a ray of sunshine streaming into his room. Susannah Lacey stood mere inches from his bed, dressed in the prettiest frock of bright yellow.

"What are you doing here?" He tried to stir from under the pillow, but his pounding head kept him lying low.

She snatched his pillow away and threw it across the room. "I am here to knock some sense into you if I have to, although I would much rather take a gentler approach."

He looked into her eyes and saw her keen interest as her gaze raked over his uncovered and completely bare upper body. What in blazes did she think she was doing? "Susannah, you must leave straightaway."

"I am not going anywhere until you give me what I want, what we both want."

She had said the words boldly, and he feared for control. She was here to tempt him, torture him. "And what is that?" he merely whispered.

"Get up out of that bed, and I shall tell you. Or I shall climb in there with you and show you."

He rolled upon his back with a groan. "Susannah," he started. "Who knows you are here? I will not let you be compromised into marriage. How foolish of you to have come here when it could seal your fate with me."

"I have told no one, and although I do like the idea of compromising you, that was not my intent in coming here." She sat down upon the end of his bed, and his pulses raced as her soft floral scent filled the air. She looked determined if not a little angry with him.

"Why have you come then? I thought I had said everything that needed to be said last night."

"You effectively tried to take my choice of the matter completely away from me." She scooted closer. "You and your puffed-up pride. Are you going to let your pride keep us apart? You have let your silly notions of noble sacrifice cloud your judgment where I am concerned, and I am quite tired of it."

He sat up and pushed himself back against the headboard of his bed, pulling what covers he could up about him as she scolded him. What she said made sense in the light of day. He had acted rashly and with stupid pride. He loved her and she loved him. That should account for far more than his lack of income.

He could not imagine what he must look like—or smell like, for that matter. He drank almost an entire bottle last night. Feeling self-conscious, he reached over, pulled out the drawer of his nightstand for a couple of cloves that he kept in a snuffbox.

"Winston! Are you listening to me?"

"Yes, and a veritable harpy you are this morning!" He popped the cloves into his mouth and chewed them quickly. He had a feeling he would be kissing her soon. "Is this what I have to look forward to? You bossing me about?"

She took that for what it was, surrender, and nearly jumped into his lap. Her arms were about his neck, and her lips were on his own. He gave in to the pleasure of holding her.

She broke their kiss and looked up into his eyes. "I love you, Winston. I want to marry you, go to India with you, and be your wife. I do not care how we shall live. I care only that we are together. Can you not see it for the grand adventure that it shall be? I care not what funds you lack when I know you will succeed with your spice business in time."

"But—" His heart was filled to overflowing as he gazed into her blue eyes. This is why she had come, to show him what he would miss without her. What he had tried to make them both miss—mornings together and nights together, like this. He had been the foolish one. They belonged together. He finally accepted that fact.

She put a finger upon his lips to quiet him. "Now, kiss me again, like you mean it."

And so he obliged her.

Susannah's heart sang as she parted her lips. She

savored the spicy taste of him. Her hands would not keep still as she touched his bare arms, shoulders, and neck. He was magnificent, and she loved the feel of his heated skin, the rough texture of his hair-spattered chest.

Somehow they had changed positions. She lay draped across him, her head upon the far pillow when he finally pulled back to gaze into her eyes. The coverlet pulled away slightly, and Susannah realized that Winston wore no bedclothes. She saw the outline of his bare hip and upper thigh. He was more beautiful than the Greek statues of Lord Elgin's Marbles. She wished that she could see him fully, when she noticed the long thin scar running along his torso. She reached out and touched it. "Is this the saber wound you received at Toulouse?"

He captured her hand and brought it to his lips, where he tenderly kissed each finger. "It is." He nibbled at her palm, and she thought she would die.

She closed her eyes and let the sensations he evoked swamp her. "Sweet torture," she murmured.

"Indeed," he whispered. He let go of her hand. "Susannah, we must talk, but I cannot begin to think clearly with you in my bed."

She opened her eyes when she felt him lift her up off of him and off of the bed.

"Please be a good girl and fetch my dressing robe over there somewhere." He pulled the coverlet back up to under his chin.

She stood on wobbly legs, her insides on fire and fluttery.

"My robe," he reminded her.

"Yes, of course. But whatever do we need to talk about?" She turned to look for the robe and tripped over his discarded boots on the floor.

"My past," he said. "Before we are wed, you must know what haunts me so that I cannot sleep. I'll not have you find out later. You may decide that you do not wish to marry such a man as me, once you hear what I have to tell you."

She turned to look at him in a moment of panic.

"There are things I have done."

And now she would hear about them.

"Very well." She squared her shoulders and handed him the heavy silk robe. Was she strong enough for this? She had to be. She would neither let her fears or sensibilities keep them apart. "Perhaps I should sit down for what you have to tell me."

"Yes, that would be best. Might I offer you tea?" he asked looking very uncomfortable as he clutched the covers and his robe at the same time.

Susannah nearly laughed with relief. It was obvious that Winston was not accustomed to entertaining ladies in his bedchamber. "No tea. Besides, I do not believe anyone is awake."

"How did you get in?" he asked.

"The window to your study was left open. I climbed in."

Winston shook his head. "Perhaps you should turn around."

She smiled despite the seriousness of their upcoming conversation. "Very well." She turned to give him privacy and focused her attention upon the floor. His coat lay in a crumpled heap, but the inside pocket revealed a hat pin. She picked it up and joy filled her. It was faded and missing a paste jewel or two, but it was the same pin she had given Winston three years ago, when they had parted. She twirled back around, catching a glimpse of Winston's bare back as he slouched into his robe. "You kept it," she said as she held it up for him to see.

He sat down next to her, taking her hands into his own. "I carried it with me always," he whispered.

She gazed at him, loving what she saw. His hair was rumpled, and his chin showed the growth of new beard upon his skin. "Winston, you did love me. All this time."

He stroked her cheek, then he took the pin from her and set it upon the small table. "I suppose that I did. But you deserved so much more than what I could offer you."

"But I only want you. You are all I have ever wanted," she whispered. She let her gaze wander away from his eyes. The robe he wore did not reach the floor. She was able to view two very well-formed legs with muscled calves leading to a pleasantly perfect pair of bare male feet.

"Are you finished ogling me, madam?" he asked with a twinkle in his eye.

"You are truly well formed," she said, feeling her cheeks grow warm.

"Thank you," he touched the end of her nose with his fingertip and whispered, "you are exquisitely formed."

She felt her blush deepen, and then her gaze strayed to the bed. What if they were to . . .

He read her thoughts instantly. "Do not tempt me any further, my lovely vixen," he warned and let go of her hands. "I am humbled by your love, and I promise to do my best to be deserving of it, but I must share with you why I have my doubts."

She snapped her gaze back to his eyes. "Then tell me."

He let out a deep sigh and sat back. "It was my first assignment. Castlereagh was suspicious. He did not believe Napoleon would accept defeat at Toulouse. And so I was sent to find a French courier and intercept the correspondence believed to be between Napoleon and his supporters." He paused.

Susannah realized that she was quite literally on the edge of her seat. "Go on." She could not imagine the horrors that Winston must have faced—both in battle and afterward as a spy.

"I was ordered to be bold, not subtle. Castlereagh wanted to send a strong message with my interception of the courier, one that clearly announced that England was watching. I was ordered to take the correspondence and kill the messenger."

She gasped, but Winston did not hear her. He was lost in a memory that pained him—haunted him. She sat with bated breath as he paused to gather his courage.

"The man I had been instructed to follow was a small Frenchman, a servant of some fine house. I followed him for days. But he was never alone. That caution proved that he knew the game. He was careful. Finally, he made a bold move and headed toward what I assumed as Elba. And I followed him."

He leaned forward and braced his elbows upon his knees while he raked his fingers through his hair. "I ambushed him. He was easy to best physically due to my size. I had him in my grasp, ready to break his neck. He fought back the best he could." Winston raised his left hand, the one with the hideous scar. "He bit me, Susannah, he locked his teeth into my flesh and would not let go. He was completely terrified. That should have been my first clue, but I paid no heed. I choked the life out of him until he finally let go in death. I searched his pockets, but there was no correspondence for Napoleon."

Susannah sat horrified. Winston had killed a man with his bare hands. She stared at the back of his left hand and the scar she had often wondered about, and shuddered.

"He was a rich merchant's servant carrying a love letter to an adulterous woman of royalty. I found the love letter on him and that was all." His eyes were bleak and filled with self-loathing.

She was up from her chair in a trice to kneel at his feet. She grabbed hold of his hands. "But you could not have known, you were instructed to seek him out and kill him." She trembled at the thought that her country could be so ruthless to instruct him so.

"I did not search him first. I could have subdued him and searched for the documents first. Instead, I killed an innocent man!" He let her hands drop and stood. He walked to the window, his back to her. He was bitterly ashamed of his actions, his remorse so great that it touched her deeply. She knelt there upon the floor, unsure how to approach him, unsure of the words to use that would ease his guilt.

"But, Winston, you said that he took great caution, as if he knew how to play the game. How could you have known otherwise? Perhaps, he truly was working for Napoleon and led you on a wild-goose chase while the real documents were sent another way."

Winston let his forehead rest against the cool glass. He was impressed by her quick mind, since it was what he had thought before he knew better. He shook his head, but did not turn to look at her. "No, Susannah, I checked. He was nothing more than a servant on a fool's errand. I never caught up with the real courier in time, and you know what resulted from there. A hundred days worth of fighting that ended in Waterloo, the worse bloodbath England had ever seen."

He felt her behind him as she wrapped her arms around his waist, leaning her head upon his back. "Winston, you could not have known, nor could you have stopped Napoleon single-handedly. You did what you had been instructed to do. What did Castlereagh have to say in the matter?"

He turned in her embrace and twined his arms around her. "A mistake. Merely a mistake."

She pulled back to look at him. "There, you see?"

He gazed into her eyes, knowing that his own were filling with tears. He did not see fear or revulsion in her. In fact, she was gazing at him with a mixture of sorrow and desire that he found completely unnerving. He was overcome with emotion, with relief, love and a hundred other things going through his soul. He pulled her against him, much too close, considering his state of undress, but her forgiving acceptance of what he had done was balm to his battle-torn soul. "And this news does not change how you feel about me?" he whispered.

"Goodness, no! Oh, Winston, all this time you feared I would hate you for what you had done? I cannot say that I like it; in fact, it chills me to the very bone, but I know that in the time of war men must do horrible things. How can I fault you for something you did in the name of duty to your country? You obeyed orders. He was the enemy, and you did what you had to do."

He said nothing, but hugged her again and breathed in her scent as if it could cleanse away his sin. "I have shared this with no other. I feared I would see the same loathing in you that I have seen in my brother's wife. I did not want that for us. I could not have borne it if you looked at me that way."

He felt her snuggle closer to him, and she kissed his neck. He was lost.

"Never, Winston. I love you. Nothing you have done or could do will change that." Then she kissed his mouth, and he groaned with wanting her. He longed to banish his past with memories of loving her, but he could not, not yet. He would not dishonor her.

He pulled back from her swollen lips and untwined her arms from around his neck. "We shall go to Sheldrake straightaway and ask permission for a special license to wed." She was a warm, wanton thing that would not let go of him. Her eyes had taken on a dreamy quality. He did not trust himself should they remain in his bedchamber much longer.

"Susannah," he said with exasperation. "You must let go of me and let me get dressed."

"You will marry me?" she asked.

"Yes, if you will have me, poor pauper that I am."

"I see how well you dress; you cannot be completely depleted of funds." Susannah stood with one hand on her hip and a saucy expression upon her face.

"I have a small account with the Bank of England, but I doubt there is enough there to buy more than five dresses in the style that you wear," he said.

"Then you may keep me at home, completely naked. It is, after all, quite hot in India." She grinned at him, and he felt his insides quake.

"You are a naughty miss. Now, go out that door while I change." He playfully slapped her bottom as she turned to leave.

"Oh!" But then she laughed, and Winston thought

it the most wonderful sound in the world. She was right. They could do without and live simply for a few years.

Susannah was bursting with happiness when she walked into the breakfast room with Winston. She vowed that he looked more at peace and carefree than she had ever seen him.

"Good morning, Susannah. My goodness, Captain Jeffries, when did you arrive?" Olivia asked.

"Just now."

"I see." Olivia turned to look at Susannah with raised eyebrows.

Susannah ignored her sister's look. "Where is Sheldrake?"

"I am here," Sheldrake said as he entered the room and snatched a muffin off of his wife's plate.

"Winston has something to ask you," Susannah blurted.

Winston pulled at her hand, "Do be quiet and let me," he said between clenched teeth.

"Finally going to offer for her, are you?" Sheldrake buttered the stolen muffin, then poured himself coffee.

Winston shook his head. This was not the way he had planned the thing to go. He wanted to ask Lord Sheldrake privately, where he could make his case and explain the situation with his military post. But both he and his wife were waiting for his answer. He looked at Susannah. She beamed at him, obviously not caring how it was done. He would not let her down. "Yes," he answered without taking his gaze away from hers. "I should very much like to offer for Susannah Lacey and make her my wife."

"And you'll be needing a special license is that it?" Lord Sheldrake asked with a wink toward his wife.

"Yes, my lord. That is exactly what we shall need."

"Very well. We can draw up the marriage settlements this afternoon."

Susannah let out a peal of laughter. She let go of his hand to run and throw herself into her brother-in-law's opened arms. In no time, Lady Sheldrake joined them, and Winston felt the most fortunate man alive as he watched the three of them embrace. He would do his very best to make Susannah happy. He finally realized that all he need do is love her completely for always.

"Lord Ponsby," a voice belonging to the butler cut through the joyous air.

Winston turned in surprise.

"I hoped that you would be here when I found your town house empty this early," Ponsby explained.

A feeling of relief cut through Winston. If Ponsby had called earlier, he and Susannah would have been in the suds.

"Join us for breakfast, Lord Ponsby. Winston has just offered for my hand in marriage and has been accepted," Susannah said.

Ponsby slapped him on his back. "Good show, old boy, good show. You will especially like what I have to tell you. After last night, when you mentioned what Castlereagh had said about your post, I managed to have a word with my future father-in-law."

Winston nodded.

"Dunsford's got some pull with Prinny, and he promised to use that on your behalf. You will get your post, I am quite sure of it. Dashed improper for Castlereagh to renege on his word."

The news hit Winston like a wave of warm water. It washed over him with pleasure and deep satisfaction. "Ponsby, I don't know how I can possibly thank you, for everything." He shook his friend's hand.

"Purely selfish intentions," Ponsby said, looking a bit embarrassed. "I cannot have my partner worry about his situation when he has a business to turn around. Consider it a mere investment toward our mutual success."

Winston nodded, but he felt suspiciously thick in the throat and did not trust himself to speak. He had been given so much when he had so little to give in return that he felt truly humbled. He looked at Susannah, his sunshine and reason for being, and knew that perhaps Destiny had shined on them after all.

Lord Sheldrake raised his cup of coffee in a toast. "To the happy couple."

"Hear, hear," they cheered.

And Susannah's gaze connected with his. He knew they would indeed be happy, for he believed what she had told him. It did not matter where they lived as long as they were together.

Author's Note

I hope you enjoyed Winston and Susannah's story. I took fictional license in a couple of areas. I found very little description of Lord Elgin's estate of Burlington House on Park Lane. I completely made up the garden maze in order to allow my characters a few private moments.

The idea for Winston's occupation stemmed primarily from my interest in the Secret Service. Being a huge James Bond fan, I wanted to create a hero who dabbled in the art of spying. Captain Winston Jeffries surprised me by not liking any of it.

In the course of my research, I received information from the Foreign & Commonwealth Office that stated during the sixteenth century, the Royal Post was in fact used to gain information by secretly intercepting correspondence of persons of interest to the government. In the seventeenth century, the government set up a regular system for clandestine interception and decryption of internal and foreign correspondence.

Eventually, major European powers were well aware of the existence of the British Secret and Decyphering Offices. Foreign governments occasionally sent misleading information by post in the expectation that the letter(s) would in fact be intercepted and the contents read. During the wars with Napoleon, both funding and British intelligence operations increased greatly. My thanks to Kate, for sending me the history notes covering the Foreign Office and the Secret Vote from 1782–1909.

I took liberty in portraying a fictionalized account of British intelligence operations during the Regency period within the above framework. The assignment I chose to give Winston was purely fictional.

Best wishes,
Jenna Mindel